A Powerful Story Mixed
With Science and Sex

THREE GO BACK

By

J. Leslie Mitchell

a complete Science Fiction Novel

GALAXY PUBLISHING CORP.
421 Hudson Street
New York 14, N. Y.

GALAXY *Science Fiction* Novels, selected by the editors of GALAXY *Science Fiction* Magazine, are the choice of science fiction novels both original and reprint.

GALAXY *Science Fiction* Novel No. 15
35c a copy. Subscription: Six Novels $2.00

PRINTED IN THE UNITED STATES OF AMERICA
by
THE GUINN COMPANY
NEW YORK 14, N. Y.

CHAPTER ONE—*The wreck of "Magellan's Cloud"* ·

A SKYEY monster, lapis and azure-blue, it sailed out of the heat-haze that all morning had been drifting westward from the Bay of Biscay. It startled the crew of the Rio tramp and there was a momentary scurry of grimy off-watches reaching the deck, and a great upward gape of astounded eyes and mouths. Then the second engineer, a knowledgeable man, voiced explanations.

"It'll be the airship *Magellan's Cloud* on her return voyage."

The Third spat, not disparagingly, but because the fumes of the engine-room were still in his throat. "Where to?"

"Man, you're unco' ignorant. Noo York. She's been lying off for weather at Paris nearly a week, Sparks says. Twenty o' a crew and twenty passengers—they'll be paying through the nose, I'll warrant. . . . There's Sparks gabbin' at her."

A subdued buzz and crackle. A tapping that presently ceased. High up against a cloudless sky, the airship quivered remoter in the Atlantic sunshine. The Third spat again, forgetfully.

"Pretty thing," he said.

The Rio tramp chugged northeastward. One or two of the crew still stood on deck, watching the aerial voyageur blend with the August sunhaze and the bubble walls of seascape till it disappeared.

And that was the last the world ever saw of the *Magellan's Cloud.*

CLAIR STRANLAY could not forget her fiancé who had died on the wire outside Mametz.

A series of chance encounters and casual conversations overhead had filled out in tenebrous vignettes each letter of the cryptic notice, Killed in Action. He had died very slowly and reluctantly, being a boy and anxious to live, and unaware that civilization has its prices. .·. . And at intervals, up into the coming of the morning, they had heard him calling in delirium: "Clair! *Oh, Clair!*"

Fourteen years ago. And still a look, a book, a word could set in motion the little disks of memory in her mind, and his voice, in its own timbre and depth and accent, would come ringing to her across the years in that cry of agony. . . . She thought, stirring from the verge of sleep in her chair of the *Magellan's* deserted passengers' lounge, "What on earth made me think of that now?"

". . . No, madam, quite definitely I've nothing to say about my deportation from Germany."

"Oh, please, Doctor Sinclair, do give your side of the case. Just a part. I'm Miss Kemp of the C. U. P., you know."

"I've nothing to say. And I'll be obliged if you'll stop pestering me."

"Oh, very well."

An angry staccato of heel taps broke out and approached. Clair, deep in her basket-chair, saw the doorway to the swinging galley blind for a moment its glimpse of ultramarine skyscape. Miss Kemp, short, sandy, stocky, stood with flushed face, biting her lips inelegantly. Then, catching sight of Clair, she came across the cabin. Clair thought, with an inward groan, "Oh, my good God, now I am in for it."

She closed her eyes, as if dozing. Unavailingly. The near basket-chair creaked under the ample, svelte-molded padding of Miss Kemp.

"Hear me try the beast? You're not asleep, are you? . . . Hear his answers? But I'll give him a write-up that'll make him and his precious league squirm, though. Dirty deportee."

"Dirty what?" Clair opened reluctant eyes.

"Deportee. Haven't you heard of him?"

"Quite likely. Who is he?"

"Why, Keith Sinclair, the agitator who's been traveling about Europe organizing the League of Militant Pacifists. Says that another war's inevitable with the present drift of things."

"Sounds logical." Clair thought: "And I hope I sound bored enough. . . . No result? Oh, well." Aloud: "And what happened?"

"Haven't you heard? He was kicked out of Italy a month ago and deported from Germany last week."

"What fun! And where's he going now?"

"Beast. To jail, I hope. Returning to America in a hurry to attend some demonstration in Boston." Miss Kemp's chair creaked its relief as she rose. "Hear that Sir John Mullaghan's on board?"

"Never heard of him at all."

"Oh, you *must* have. Awfully important. Conservative M. P. Head of the armaments people. I'm off to get his opinion of the trip. Rather amusing, you know; he and Sinclair have met before."

"Have they?"

"Didn't you hear? Awful shindy. Sir John was making a speech at some place in Berlin. Said there would always be wars and that honest men prepared for them. Sinclair stood up in the audience and interrupted and started a speech of his own. Police had to interfere, and that led to his deportation. Sinclair's, I mean. Wonder if Sir John knows he's on board the *Magellan?*"

"I haven't heard."

"Will be a scoop if they say anything when they meet! Did you hear
—oh, there's Sir John crossing to the steering cabin. I'll get him now."

Clair cautiously raised the eyelids below her penciled brows. Like
talking to the bound files of the *News-Chronicle*. The lounge was empty,
the passengers in their cabins or on the galleries. Miss Kemp's high-
heeled footfalls receded. . . . Blessed relief.

That article in *Literary Portraits* Miss Kemp had written about her,
had been sheer claw, Clair remembered.

BEST-SELLER FROM THE SLUMS

Miss Clair Stranlay, whose real name is Elsie Moggs . . . born in
a tenement house in Battersea . . . best-seller in England and
America. . . .

Most of it true enough, of course. Except for the Elsie Moggs bit. A
bad mixup that on Miss Kemp's part when searching out antecedents
in Thrush Road. She'd missed the story of how fond Stranlay *mère* had
been of novelettes—even to the extent of christening her daughter out
of one of them. . . .

Romance! Romance that had beckoned so far away beyond the
kindly poverty of Thrush Road!

"My dear girl, you came on this voyage for rest, not reminiscence."

But not even the *Magellan's* soothing motion could recapture that
drowsiness from which the sound of Miss Kemp's attempted interview-
ing had evicted her. She thought, with a laggard curiosity, "Wonder if
the Sinclair man is the one with the beard and false front who ate so
hard at lunch? Throat-cutting is probably hungry work. Let's look."

And, as idly as that, she was afterward to reflect, she stood up and
strolled out of the *Magellan's* lounge and out of the twentieth century.

BELOW her, trellis-work of wood and aluminum and, in the interstices, the spaces of the sun-flooded ocean. The beat of the engines
astern sounded remote and muffled. There was not a cloud.

Then, raising her eyes, she saw Keith Sinclair for the first time. He
turned with blown hair at the moment, glancing at her uninterestedly,
looked away, looked back again.

He saw a woman who might have been anything from twenty-five to
thirty years of age, and who, as a matter of data, was thirty-three. She
was taller than most men liked, with that short-cut, straight brown hair
which has strands and islets of red in it. And indeed, that red spread

to her eyelashes, which were very long, though Sinclair did not discover this until afterward, and to her eyes, which had once been blue before the gold-red came into them. Nose and chin, said Sinclair's mind methodically, very good, both of them. She can breathe, which is something. Half the women alive suffer from tonsillitis. But that mouth . . . And he definitely disapproved of the pursed, long-lipped mouth in the lovely face—the mouth stained scarlet.

"Weather keeping up," said Clair helpfully.

He said, "Yes."

She thought, "My dear man, I don't want to interview you. Only to collect you as a comic character. Sorry you haven't that beard."

Nearly six feet three inches in height, too long in the leg and too short in the body. All his life, indeed, there had been something of the impatient colt in his appearance. He had a square head and gray eyes set very squarely in it; high cheek-bones, black hair, and the bleached white hands of his craft. Those hands lay on the gallery railing now.

"Wish I could go and smoke somewhere," said Clair.

"So do I."

"A little ambiguous."

He stared rudely.

Clair said suddenly, "Goodness!"

Startled, they both raised their heads.

The metal stays below their feet had swung upward and downward, with a soggy swish of imprisoned lubricant. The whole airship had shuddered and for a moment had seemed to pause, so to speak, in its stride. Sinclair leaned over the gallery railing.

"Hell, look at the sea."

Clair looked. The Atlantic was boiling. Innumerable maelstroms were rising from the depths, turning even in that distance below them from bluegreen to white, creamed white, and then, in widening ripples, to dark chocolate. Clair felt a prick of interest in the performance.

"What's causing it?"

The American was silent for a moment, regarding the Atlantic with a scowl of surprise. He said, "Impossible."

"What is?"

"I said impossible." He brushed past her toward the doorway of the lounge. Paused. "See the dark chocolate?"

Clair nodded, regarding him with a faint amusement.

"Well, don't you see it must have come from the bottom?"

"So it must." She peered down again. "And it's deep here, isn't it?"

"Perhaps a couple of miles." He disappeared.

News of the submarine earthquake spread quickly enough. Passengers crowded the galleries.

"The chocolate's dying away," said Clair Stranlay.

So it was. The Atlantic had resumed its natural hue. The maelstroms had vanished, or the airship had passed beyond the locality where they still uprose. For, after that first shudder, the *Magellan's Cloud* had held on her way unfalteringly. The snapshotter beside Clair wrinkled a puzzled brow.

"Very strange. I could have sworn there was a ship down there to the south only a minute or so ago. It's disappeared. . . . Quick going."

The airship beat forward into the waiting evening. Sky and sea were as before. But presently there gathered in the west such polychrome splendor of sunset as the *Magellan's* commander, who had crossed the Atlantic many times by ship, had never before observed.

And suddenly, inexplicably, it grew amazingly cold.

THE airship's wireless operator fumed over dials and board, abandoned the instrument, went out into the miniature crow's nest that overhung his cabin, glanced about him and beat his hands together in the waft of icy air that chilled them.

"Damn funny," he commented.

He went back to his cabin and rang up the *Magellan's* commander. The latter had donned the only overcoat he had brought on board and was discussing the weather with the navigator when the wireless operator's voice spoke in his ear.

"Is that you, sir?"

"Yes."

"I'm sorry, but it seems impossible to send that message."

"Eh?"

"I thought there was some fault in the set. I've been sitting here for the last two and a half hours trying to tap in on France or a ship. There's no message come through. I've sent out yours, but there's been no reply."

The commander was puzzled. "That's strange, Gray. Sure your instrument is functioning all right?"

"Certain, sir. I've broadcast to the receiving apparatus in the passengers' lounge and they heard perfectly."

"Damn funny. Get it right as soon as you can, will you?"

"But . . . right, sir."

The commander put down the telephone and turned to give the news to the navigator. They were in the steering cage and it was just after

eight o'clock. But the navigator, instead of standing by with his usual
stolid lack of expression was at the far end of the cage, staring upward.

"Gray says the infernal wireless has gone out of order. Bright lookout
if we go into fog over the banks. . . . Hello, anything wrong?"

"Come here, Commodore."

The commander crossed to the navigator's side. The latter pointed
up to a darkling sky which, ever since the sudden fall of temperature,
had been adrift with a multitude of cloudlets.

"Look. Up there."

"Only the moon. Well?"

"Well, it's only the twenty-second. The new moon, in its first quarter,
isn't due till the twenty-seventh. And that one's gibbous."

"Good Christopher!"

They both stared at the sky through the lattice of airship wire, amazed,
half-convinced that some trick was being played upon them. From behind the clouds the moon was indeed emerging, round and wind-flushed
and full. It sailed the sky serenely, five days ahead of time, taking stock
of this other occupant of its firmament. The *Magellan's* commander
brought his glasses to bear on it. It appeared to be the same moon.

"But it's impossible. The calendar must be wrong."

"The only thing possibly wrong is the date. And it's not—as of course
we know. Look, here's to-day's *Matin.*"

He showed it. It was dated the twenty-second of August, 1932.

The airship *Magellan's Cloud* beat forward into the growing radiance
of moonlight which had mysteriously obliterated the last traces of day.

LOOKING out from his cabin window as he prepared to undress and
go to bed, the American, Keith Sinclair, was startled. He was aware
that it had grown intensely cold, as indeed was every soul on board the
Magellan's Cloud, whether on duty or in bed. But now his gaze revealed
to him the fact that the airship's hull was silvered with frost in the
moonlight. Frost at this altitude in August?

For a moment he accepted the moonlight. And then standing in the
soft *hush-hush* of the flexible airship walls, realization of the impossibility of that moon came on him, as it had done on the navigator.

"Now how the devil did you come to be there?"

The moon, sailing a sky that was now quite clear, cloudless and star-
less, made no answer. The notorious deportee whistled a little, remembering a Basque story heard from his mother—of how the sun one morning had risen in the semblance of the moon. . . . But that didn't help.
It wasn't nearly morning yet. And it was an indubitable moon.

Still whistling, he felt his pulse and, as an afterthought, took his temperature. Both were normal. Meanwhile, the cold increased. Sinclair pulled open his cabin door.

"Look up the navigator again. He had precious little explanation of that submarine earthquake, but the moon's beyond ignoring."

But, crossing the lounge, a glimpse of the dark seascape beyond the open door drew him out on the passengers' gallery. There it was even colder, though there was no gale. The ship was traveling at a low altitude. Below, smooth, vast and unhurrying, the rollers of the Atlantic passed out of the near sheen of moonlight into the dimness astern. . . . Abruptly Sinclair became aware that the gallery had another occupant.

Clair Stranlay: in pajamas, slippers and wrap. Intent on the night and the sea. The American groped along the hand-rail toward her.

"Feel ill?"

She started. "What? Doctor Sinclair, isn't it? I'm quite well."

"You'll be down with pneumonia if you stay here."

"Don't think so. I do winter bathing and icy baths. What's happened?"

"The cold?"

"Yes."

"Early bergs down from the north, I suppose."

"But it's not nearly the season yet."

He had seen something in the moonlight below them.

Out of the deserted Atlantic was emerging what appeared to be an immense berg—a sailing of cragged, shapeless grayness upon the water. The moonlight struck wavering bands of radiance from it, and for a moment, in some trick of refraction, it glowed a pearled blue as though lighted from within. It passed underfoot, and as it passed a beam of light shot down from the navigating cabin, played upon it, passed, returned, hesitated, hovered, was abruptly extinguished.

But not so quickly that the two occupants of the passengers' gallery failed to see an accretion such as no iceberg ever bore. For beyond the berg had showed up a long, sandy beach, and beyond that the vague suggestion, of a flat and comberwashed island.

Sinclair swore, unimpassioned. "I'm going to find out about this. Are we making for the Pole?"

Clair, something to her own amusement, found herself shaking with excitement. "But what could it have been? There are no islands on the France-New York track."

"We've just seen one. I'm going to find out what the navigating cabin knows about it. Unless we're Pole-bound—and that's nonsense—the submarine earthquake may have thrown it up."

"It must have done other things as well, then." Clair began to stamp her feet to warmth. The rest of her felt only the glow of well-being that falling temperatures nowadays gifted her unfailingly as guerdon for much braving of wintry dips. "Haven't you noticed something entirely missing from the sea—even though this is the crowded season?"

"What?" He sounded impatient.

"Ship-lights. Not one has shown up since sunset."

"Who said so?"

"One of the riggers I spoke to just now."

She saw, dimly, his puzzled scowl.

"The submarine quake we saw couldn't have affected shipping. It was quite localized. If it had caused great damage the wireless bulletins they post in the lounge would have told us."

The same thought occurred to them simultaneously. Clinging to the handrail, she followed Sinclair into the cabin. The case with wireless transcriptions was hung against the farther wall. They crossed to it, looked at it and then looked at each other.

No notices had been posted since five.

"Look here, Miss—"

"Stranlay."

"Miss Stranlay, I'm going to find out about things. Something extraordinary seems to have happened. But if any of the other passengers come out, don't alarm them."

"I alarm people only in my books."

"Oh! Do you write?"

"Novels."

"Oh! I'd go to bed if I were you. I'll tap on your cabin door and let you know what I hear."

Passing through the hull, he stopped at a window and himself noted another happening.

The moonlight was pouring lengthwise into the long hull of *Magellan's Cloud*, not striking due in front, as a moment before.

The airship had turned southward.

CLAIR STRANLAY arrived in her cabin, and, looking out at the far moon-misted horizon of the Atlantic, she thought:

"He'd never heard of me! Publicity, where are thy charms? . . . Any more than I of him. But how desperately important folk we are to ourselves!"

A spear-beam of white moonlight splashed on her shoulder and she raised her head, and looked at it. She put up her hand.

"The blessed thing feels almost cold."

Something quite extraordinary had happened to the *Magellan's Cloud*. But what? Delay it much reaching New York?

"Oh, my good God!" sighed Clair, getting into bed.

For, escaping England and boredom to go and lecture in America, the awfulness of the ennui, hitherto concealed, that lay awaiting her appalled her. The shore. Miles and miles of ferroconcrete, macadam, pelting rush and automobilist slither. Packing of clothes. Custom shed. Forms. Beefy officials. Forms. Literary gatherings. And rows and rows of eyes set in faces more like those of paralytic codfish than human beings.

And, thinking of them, Clair's mind-mask of insouciance, brittle and bright, quivered and almost showered her soul with its flakes. Sometimes, indeed, it cracked and fell about her entirely, and she'd hear that boy on the wire outside Mametz, and her desperate distaste for her work, her life and her century crescendoed in her heart. . . .

"Oh, forget it. The mess of our lives! Civilization! Ragged automatons or lopsided slitherers."

But here Clair Stranlay found the blessedness of sleep now close upon her. Her body had lost its surface cold. She curled up her toes a little under the quilt—they were even, uncramped and shapely toes—and sighed a little, and fell fast asleep—and was shot out of sleep five minutes later by a knock at the door of her cabin.

"YES, come in," she called, good-tempered even then: good temper had dogged her through life. Was it morning already and had they sighted New York?

But there was no daylight, only moonlight, entering the cabin window. She reached up to the switch and in the pallor of electric light looked at the American. Keith Sinclair, shutting the door, thought, "Pretty thing."

"About what's happened, Miss Stranlay— Can I sit down?"

"Why, yes," said Clair, blinking her eyes. "There's a chair."

The American sat down. His high-cheeked-boned face was dourly thoughtful. "We're in this together in a fashion, I suppose, seeing we were the first to see the submarine quake. Well—the commander refused to talk sense. Scared I will alarm the others, I suppose. But he has to admit that no wireless messages have been received since the time of the submarine disturbance, though the apparatus of the *Magellan* appears to be perfectly in order. Also, he's turned the airship south."

"South?" Clair's hands dropped from her neck at that. "Then we're not making New York?"

"We're not," grimly. "We'll be lucky if we fetch up in Brazil at this rate."

"Thank God," said Clair.

"Eh?"

"Nothing. Not particularly anxious to reach New York. The codfish can wait. . . . Sorry, I'm still half asleep. Nice of you to come and tell me the news. Why has the *Magellan* turned south, then, and what does the captain say about that island with the berg we saw from the gallery?"

"Turned south because he's scared about the effect of the continued cold on the airship's envelope. I don't wonder, either. I met your garrulous rigger just now and he says we're carrying tons of ice. As for the island—the navigator says we're mistaken."

"Astigmatism or too much liquor?"

He grinned—a softening relaxation. "Neither in his case and both in ours, he seems to think. Truth of the matter is that the crew is as puzzled as we are, but they think if the passengers knew they'd blame them for all these extraordinary phenomena. There's another thing, Miss Stranlay, which you didn't notice. The most serious of the lot. It's the moon."

"What has it done?"

"Arrived five days ahead of time. There shouldn't be a full moon for another fortnight; there shouldn't be a moon at all just now."

"But—that *is* the moon."

He looked through the cabin window at it. "It is." He rubbed his chin impatiently. "And it isn't. . . . Eh?"

"I said, clear as mud."

"Oh! It's a thing not easy to explain." He stood up. "But I've a telescope with me—probably the most powerful magnifier on the *Magellan* —and I've had a peek at the moon through it. Just a minute."

He was back in less. He opened the cabin window and poised the telescope on the ledge. Clair sat forward and looked through it.

"Keep both eyes open," advised the American.

So she did, and for a moment was blinded in consequence. The moon was sinking. Stars were appearing pallidly. Clair gazed across space.

"Nothing very different, is it? I've looked at it through the big glass at Mount Wilson. Why—the nose!"

The Man in the Moon lacked a nose. Clair turned her face to Sinclair's moon-illumined one. He nodded.

"Exactly. That mountain range on the moon is missing. Something is happening up there."

She thought for a moment, caught a glimpse of a possible explanation. "Then—the tides are caused by the moon. Mayn't the submarine earthquake have been caused by the change in the moon?"

"Perhaps. I'm not an astronomer. But something abnormal has happened to the moon—both to her surface and her rate of revolution. The submarine earthquake we witnessed may have been the result. Probably it's had other effects in the far north—God knows what."

"And the wireless interruptions due to the same cause?" Clair Stranlay lowered the telescope from her cabin-window in the *Magellan*. "Most interesting thing I've seen for years. Pity we've explained it all so nicely."

But, as they were later to learn, they were very far indeed from having explained it.

A ND presently, while Clair slept again and Sinclair tried to sleep and the commander sat peering at an almanac, and the navigator peered into the west—a pale shimmer of daylight arose in the east, lighting the surface of that strange Atlantic, flowing liquid almost as the Atlantic itself till it touched the southward-hasting, high-slung cars of the *Magellan's Cloud*. A moment it lingered (as if puzzled) on that floating monster of the wastes, and then, abruptly, was snuffed out.

And the navigator from his gallery was shouting urgent directions into the engine-room telephone.

It is doubtful if they ever reached the engineers. For at that moment the nose of the *Magellan*, driving south at the rate of eighty miles an hour, rustled and crumpled up with a thin crack of metallic sheathing. The whole airship sang in every strut and girder, and, quivering like a stunned bird, still hung poised against the mountain range that had arisen out of the darkness.

The drumming roar roused to frantic life everyone on board, asleep or awake. Most of the passengers probably succeeded in leaving their beds, if not their cabins. On the lurching floors of these they may have caught horrified glimpses of the next moment's happening.

The airship's hull spurted into bright flames, green-glowing, long-streaming in the darkness that had succeeded the false twilight. Then the whole structure broke apart, yet held together by the tendrils of the galleries and cabins, and, like an agonized, mutilated thing, drew back from the mountainside and fell and flamed and fell again, unendingly, in two long circles. . . .

And then suddenly the Atlantic yawned and hissed, while the dawn passed overhead and lighted the mountains and hastened into the west.

CHAPTER TWO—*The survivors*

NOW, what happened to Clair Stranlay in that dawn-wrecking of the
Magellan's Cloud was this:

The preliminary shock, when the nose of the airship drove into the
mountain which had mysteriously arisen out of the spaces of the Atlantic, did not awaken her. She stirred uneasily, though still asleep,
during the period that the *Magellan* hung, death-quivering, against her
murderer. Then, abruptly, sight, hearing and a variety of other sensa-
tions were vouchsafed to her fortissimo, crescendo.

She heard the first explosion which shattered the hull of the airship,
and leaped up in bed to see through the cabin window, phantasmagoric
against a gray morning sky, the flare and belch of the flames. She sat
stunned, uncomprehending, the while the floor of her cabin tilted and
tilted and the metal-work creaked and warped. Then the cabin door, a
groaning, flare-illumined panel, was torn open, a figure shot in, crossed
to Clair's bed and caught her with rough hands. It was Sinclair.

"Come on, hurry up! The ship's a flaming wreck. . . ."

He swept a pile into his arms from the locker. Clair jumped from
bed, plucked something—she could not see what it was—from the floor,
and groped across the cabin after Sinclair. He tugged at the door. It
had jammed.

Now, out of the corridor, above the babel of sounds, one sound
sharp-edged and clear came to them: a moan like that of trapped cattle.
For a moment it rang in Clair's ears in all its horror, and then—the floor
of the cabin vanished from beneath the feet of Sinclair and herself.

Below, the Atlantic.

And Clair thought, "Oh God," and fell and fell, with a flaming comet
in wavering pursuit. Till something that seemed like a red-hot dagger
was thrust to the hilt into her body.

BREAKERS, and breakers again—the cry of them and the splash of
them, and their salt taste stale in her mouth. In and in, and out with
a slobbering surge. Water in pounding hill-slopes, green and white-
crested. Pounding tons of water whelming over into those breakers. . . .
Clair Stranlay cried out and awoke.

"Better? I thought you'd gone. . . . My God, look at the *Magellan!*"

Her body seemed wrapped in a sheet of fire that was a sheet of ice.
She could not open her eyes. She tried again. They seemed fast-gummed.
Then, abruptly, they opened. She moaned at the prick of the salt-grime.

She and Keith Sinclair were lying in a wide sweep of mountain-surrounded bay, on a beach of pebbles. Beyond and below them the sea was thundering. And out in the bay, the *Magellan's Cloud* was flaming against a dark-gray, rainy sky momentarily growing lighter, as if the *Magellan* were serving as tinder to its conflagration.

This was not what Clair saw immediately. It was what she realized as she looked around her. Sinclair lay at right angles to her.

Clair stared at him, sought for her voice, found it after an interval, manipulated it with stiff and very painful lips.

"How did we get here?"

"Swam." The American swayed to his knees. His high-cheek-boned face looked as though the blood had been drained from it through a pipette. "We hit the water before the *Magellan* did, and sank together. Came up clear of the wreck and I pulled you ashore. . . . Oh, damn!"

He felt very sick indeed. There was an inshore-blowing wind, bitterly cold. With a shock Clair discovered she was dressed in her pajamas only. Through those garments the rain-laden wind drove piercingly. It was laden now with other things than rain—adrift with red-glowing fragments of fluff, portions of the *Magellan's* fabric. The *Magellan?*

In that moment the airship blew up. A second later Clair saw its great girders, like the skeleton of a great sow, then they vanished.

The eastward sky was blinded to darkness in the flash, Clair and Sinclair momentarily stunned with the noise of the explosion. Then a great wave poured shoreward out of the stirred water of the bay, leaped up the beach, snarled, spat, soaked and splashed them anew, tore at them, retreated. Gasping, Clair saw Sinclair's hand extended toward her. She caught it.

Unspeaking, now crawling, now gaining their feet and proceeding at a shambling run, they attained the upper beach. Fifty yards away, across the shingle, there towered in the dimness of the morning great cliffs of black basalt. Against their black wall Sinclair thought he discerned a fault and overhang. He pointed toward it and they stumbled together across sharp stones that lacerated their feet. Anything to get out of the wind and spray. Clair almost fell inside the crack in the rock-face. Sinclair crumpled to the ground beside her. Clair heard some one sobbing and realized it was herself.

"What's wrong?"

She looked up at him, her teeth chattering, thinking, "I suppose we'll both be dead in a minute." She said, "I'm all right."

Prone, he began to laugh crackedly at that. Clair stuffed her fingers in her ears and looked out to sea.

It was deserted. The *Magellan's Cloud* had disappeared without leaving other trace than themselves. Green, tremendous, with tresses upraised and flying through the malachite comb of the wind, the Atlantic surged over the spot where the wreck had flamed. An urgent fear came upon Clair. She shook the American's shoulder.

"Where are the others?"

"Dead."

He had stopped laughing. He lay face downward, unmoving. Clair shook him again.

"You mustn't! You must keep awake and. . . ."

But she knew it was useless. Her own head nodded in exhaustion. She laid her face in the curve of her arm and presently was as silent as he was.

THE morning wind died away and with its passing the sky began to clear. Lying exhausted and asleep in their inadequate shelter under the lee of the cliffs the two survivors of the airship's wreck stirred at the coming of the sunlight. Sinclair awoke, sat up, looked around, remembered.

He was in pajamas. The suit clung to his skin in damp and shuddersome patches. He stood up. His feet were cut and bruised. The salt bit into them as he moved. Alternate waves of warmth and coldness flowed up and down his body .

Setting his teeth against giving way to the pull of the urgent pain in his feet, he began to knead and pound his throat and chest and abdomen and thighs, then took to massaging them, plucking out and releasing muscles like a violin-maker testing the strings of a bow. Suddenly something screamed at him, menacingly.

He glanced up, startled. It was a solitary gull. He thought, "And a peculiar one, too." It swooped and hovered, its bright eyes on the occupants of the shelter. Man and bird looked at each other unfriendlily. Then the gull, with a slow beating of wings, flapped out of sight. Sinclair resumed operations on his now tingling body.

Behind him, Clair Stranlay began to moan.

Her eyes opened at last. She sat up, remembering at once.

"Any of the others turned up?"

He shook his head. "The sunlight woke me," he told her.

"I'm horribly thirsty."

"So am I. I'll go and look for water in a minute."

"Where do you think we are?"

"Somewhere in the Bay of Biscay. Coast of Portugal, perhaps."

"People inland must have seen the wreck of the *Magellan*. They're bound to come down to the shore, aren't they?"

"Bound to, I should think. Feel certain enough to rise now?"

She stood up with his arm supporting her. Instantly, in the full sunlight, she began to shiver. He nodded.

"Warm up with exercises. Know how? Right. I'll go and look for water and see if any people are coming down the cliffs."

He went, limping blood-heeled. Clair stared after him till his black poll vanished round a projection of rock, and then emerged slowly from her sleeping-suit.

Her feet, like Sinclair's, she discovered bloody, though not so badly cut. Except its craving for water, her body in the next few strenuous minutes acquired comfort and familiarity again. The pajamas steamed in the sunlight; ceased to steam. In ten minutes they were dry.

"There's water to the left—a cascade over the rocks. Can you walk?"

She essayed the adventure gingerly. "Easily."

Out in the full sunlight she stopped to look round the bay. Desolate. The navigator, the commander, Miss Kemp—a fit of shuddering came on again. She covered her face with her hands.

But the horror lingered for a moment only, and then was gone. She turned to the American, a pace behind her, waiting for her, a grotesque figure in his shrunken pajamas, his blue-black hair untidily matted. He stood arms akimbo, scowling at the sea. A gull—there seemed but one gull in the bay—swooped over their heads.

She became aware that the silence around them was illusory. It was a thing girdled by unending sound, as the earth is girdled with ether. The tide was no longer in full flow, but the serene thunder of the breakers was unceasing.

The pebbles underfoot were slimily warm. From the sea a breath of fog was rising, like thin cigarette smoke. Not a ship or a boat was in sight, nothing upon or above the spaces of the Atlantic but a solitary cirrus low down in the northeastern sky.

They turned a corner in the winding wall of cliff and were in sight of the waterfall. In distance it seemed to hang bright, lucent, unmoving, a silver pillar in a dark pagan temple. Clair loved it for this beauty. She bent and scooped from it a double handful of water.

It was icily cold. Some drops splashed through her jacket. They stung like leaden pellets. She shivered and, squatting, rinsed her mouth and laved her face. Sinclair looked down at her; knelt down beside her. They scoured their faces in solemn unison. Standing up, Sinclair looked round about him, involuntarily, for a towel. Clair wiped her face with the sleeve of her pajamas. Sinclair followed suit. Wiping, he suddenly stayed operations.

"Here's some one at last."

He pointed toward the leftward tip of the bay. A black-clad figure was descending the inky, sun-laced escarpment, apparently less steep at that spot than elsewhere. It was descending in haste. It had descended. It stood hesitant, glancing upward, not toward them. Clair put her fingers to her mouth and startled the bay, Sinclair and the stranger with a piercing, moaning whistle which the rocks caught and echoed.

"Stop that!" said Sinclair angrily.

He was to see often enough in succeeding days that look of innocent, amused surprise on the lovely face turned toward him. The black-garmented figure had started violently, seen them, stood doubtful a moment, but now, with gesticulating arm, was coming toward them.

"I can't speak a word of Portuguese," said Clair. "Can you?"

There was a pause. Then: "It won't be necessary. I don't suppose he knows Portuguese himself."

"No?" Puzzled, Clair examined the nearing stranger. He was finding the going punishing. He stumbled. His features changed from a blur to discernible outlines. "Who is he?"

"A fellow-passenger on the *Magellan*. Sir John Mullaghan."

"I WAS washed ashore at the far peak of the bay when the *Magellan's Cloud* struck the water. I imagined I was the only survivor."

The gray-haired man with the gentle sensitive face was addressing Clair. She held out her hand to him.

"I'm Clair Stranlay. Doctor Sinclair rescued me." She glanced from one to the other, thinking, "Don't bite."

Sir John Mullaghan began to unbutton his coat. Clair said, wide-eyed. "What's wrong?"

"You must wear my coat, Miss Stranlay."

"No, thanks. I'm quite comfy. How ever do you come to be wearing your clothes?"

"I found it too cold to go to bed, and was sitting up studying some documents when the wreck occurred." His small neat form was clad in the shrunken caricature of a dress suit. Collar and tie were missing; the breast of the shirt was very limp and muddied. Sinclair glanced sidewise at his feet and scowled again. Shod in thin pumps that were at least some slight protection. . . .

Clair said, "Let's sit down. What did you see at the top of the cliff?"

"A lion. One of the largest brutes I have ever seen. It stalked me close to the cliff-head."

Clair glanced at Sinclair, glanced back at Sir John, looked up at the cliffs. "A *lion?* But I thought we were in Portugal?"

"I don't know where we are. But this is not the coast of Portugal. At the top of the cliff there is a further terrace-wall to be climbed. It is fringed with bushes and trees. I expected to get some view of the country there and went up about half an hour ago."

"What happened?"

"I pushed through the fringe of bushes until I came to a fairly open space. I was certain that I would see some village near at hand, or at least houses and some marks of cultivation." He paused. "There are no houses and the country is quite wild. It is natural open park-land, dotted with clumps of trees, stretching as far away as one can see. And on the horizon, five or six miles distant from here, are two volcanoes."

"Volcanoes?" The American was startled into speech. "You must have been mistaken."

"I have quite good eyesight."

The American bit his lip. Clair said, "Where do you think we are, then?"

"Somewhere on the coast of Africa."

"But it's much too cold. And I never heard of volcanoes on the coast of Africa."

"There are no volcanoes on the coast of Africa. Most likely the lion was some beast escaped from a menagerie."

This was Sinclair. Sir John Mullaghan flushed. Clair, wondering bemusedly if there was ever an armaments manufacturer who looked less the part, wondered also if the beast of which he spoke had had any existence outside the reaches of a disaster-strained imagination. She looked again at the cliff-top, shining in the cool sunlight. "We'll have to go up there and look for food, anyhow. I'm horribly hungry."

All three of them were. It was nearing noon. They licked hungry lips. Sinclair, peering up at the cliffs in the breaker-hung silence, thought, "Hungry? As hell. But if this patriot warrior didn't dream, there's a lion up there. Still—without food we'll never last another night."

Clair thought, "Now if this were a good novel of wrecked mariners we'd toss up for it to see which was to eat t'other." And she began to giggle, being very hungry and somewhat dizzy.

"Miss Stranlay!"

"It's all right. I was thinking of a funny story."

"Oh!"

"Yes." She stood up, suddenly decided. "Wrecked people sometimes eat each other if they can't get other food—at least, they always do in my profession. Let's climb the cliff and see if the lion's gone."

"Come on, then," said Sinclair shortly, striding over the shingle. They followed him, Sir John Mullaghan dubiously, Clair satisfiedly, and once surreptitiously trying to rub some feeling into her oddly-numbed stomach. Sinclair was making for the point ascended and descended by the armaments manufacturer. His survey of the cliffs had told him that no other spot was climbable.

They went on along the deserted beach. The tide was going out. Sinclair glanced back casually, halted in his stride, stared, abandoned the other two, strode past them.

"Wait."

THEY looked after him. Ten yards away he bent over something at the wet verge of shingle. He picked it up. It glittered, wetly. He shook it vigorously. Clair called. "What is it?"

"An eider-down quilt."

So it was. Brought nearer in Sinclair's arms, Clair recognized it.

"It's off my cabin-bed in the *Magellan!* . . . That was the thing I must have picked up when you came to get me."

"Lucky that you did."

"Why?" She regarded it without enthusiasm. "It's very wet, isn't it?"

"It'll dry. And the nights are likely to be cold."

"But—" Clair looked out to sea, looked round the deserted bay again. The possibility that this was not, after all, a few hours' lark struck her. "We'll be rescued before then."

Neither of the men spoke. Sir John passed a gray hand over his gray hair. Sinclair's comment was the usual impatient frown. . . . They resumed their progress cliffward, the barefoot refugees slipping on the moist pebbles, Sir John in slightly better case.

The bay's solitary sea-gull was following them. Clair held out her hand to it. At that, as if frightened by the gesture, it turned in the air in a wide loop, and planed away steeply down toward the retreating tide. The American was speaking to Sir John.

"We've no shoes. Will you lead?"

The armaments manufacturer hesitated only a moment, nodded curtly and began the ascent. The silence but for his scrapings over the rock was more intense than ever.

Sinclair and Clair followed, the American in a short time beginning to swear violently under his breath because of his cut feet. Clair said, "Say something for me as well."

He glanced at her—almost a puzzled glance—from below his dark unhappy brows. Then he went on. Clair, panting, poised to rest. She was more than a little frightened. Where were they? And what on earth was going to happen? And how long would her pajamas last?

Sinclair's toiling back, quilt-laden, reproached her sloth. Sir John Mullaghan had almost disappeared.

From the shore the circling gull saw the three strange animals dwindle to spider-splayed shadows against the face of the cliffs, dwindle yet further to hesitant, foreshortened dots on the cliff-brow, and then vanish forever from its ken.

CHAPTER THREE—"I'm an Unknown Land"

THREE days later, and the coming of nightfall. Almost it came in countable strides.

They had drowsed in the clear sharp sunshine that picked out so pitilessly the hilly, wooded contours of the deserted land. Swamp and plain and rolling grassland, straggling rightward forest fringe, a swamp and plain and hill again. Unendingly. But with the westerning of the sun these things had softened in outline, blurred in distance, and now, on the hesitating edge of darkness, the great chain of volcanoes lighted and lighted till they were a beckoning candelabrum, casting long shadows and gleams of light over leagues of the bleak savanna.

The coming nightfall paused a little, as if astounded by a spot in the tree-sprayed foothills that led to the volcanoes' range.

For here, in all that chilled and hushed and waiting expectancy, were three things that did not wait, that bore human heads and bodies. For three sunsets now the nightfall had come on those three hastening figures. Each time they were farther south, each time they greeted the diurnal traveler with thin ridiculous pipings in that waste land overshadowed by the volcanoes.

"'Fraid it'll beat us," said the middle figure, a short bunched shapelessness.

The leading figure, tall and hastening, grunted. The last figure, breathing heavily, said: "I also think it's useless. We had much better try the forest."

"What do you think, Doctor Sinclair?" asked the midway shapelessness.

The leader grunted again.

"Damn nonsense. We'll climb toward the volcanoes, where we've a chance of getting warm. Another night in the open may finish us. And the forest's not safe."

Underfoot, the heavy-fibered grass rustled harsh and wet to the touch of naked feet. The heavy-breathing rearward figure said:

"There is probably no danger in the forest. You saw things while you were half-awake. In daylight we've seen no animal larger than a small deer."

The leading figure swore, turned a shadowed face, halted and confronted the rear-guard, and disregarded a restraining motion made by the shapelessness. "Damn you and your impertinences. Did you imagine that lion you originally saw, then?"

And the middle shapelessness which, under the endrapement of the eiderdown quilt salvaged from the wreck of the *Magellan's Cloud*, contained Clair Stranlay, thought, "Goodness, they're both nearly all in. What on earth am I to do if they start scrapping now?"

That question had vexed her almost continually for some seventy hours. The American and Sir John Mullaghan had seemed to her designed from the beginning of the world to detest each other. For seventy hours they had adjusted fairly well, but she'd known antagonism would show. And now—

Clair thought, "Oh my good God, I could knock your silly heads together. And I'm cold and miserable and hungry. And if ever we get out of this awful country I'll write an account and lampoon you both—"

THERE would be plenty of copy for that account. . . . The wreck. The rescue. Sir John Mullaghan arriving on the scene, complete with tale of discourteous lion. Climbing the cliffs. No lion. Wide view of the sea. No ships. No food. And before them an unrecognizable landscape about which Sinclair and Sir John had at once begun to disagree. Labrador or North Canada, said Sinclair—abruptly deserting Portugal. There were supposed to be lost volcanoes in the wilds of Canada. Sir John had asked if there were also lions, and how the *Magellan*, turning south just prior to being wrecked, could have reached Canada? No reply to that. Scowls. All three growing hungry. Finally, exploration in search of food.

It had led them farther and farther inland, that exploration. No animals. Not a solitary bird. Strange land without the sound of birds, without the chirp of grasshoppers in those silent forest clumps! Clair had shivered at that voicelessness, though, far off beyond the cliffs, they could still hear the moan of the lost Atlantic.

They had strayed remoter and remoter from that moan, out into thinner aspects of the park-land, till the landscape they saw was this: Distant against the eastern horizon a long mountain sierra, ivory-toothed with snow, cold and pale and gleaming in the cool sunshine, except at points lighted with the lazy smoking of volcanoes. To the right a jumble of hills that must lead back to the Atlantic, and those hills matted and clogged with forest. But no jungle. Pines and conifers and firs.

"Likely-looking country for lion," the American remarked acidly, and then hushed them both with a sharp gesture. Something stirred in a clump of bushes only a yard or so away. They'd stared at it, making out at last the head and shoulders and attentive antlers of a small deer. Sinclair had acted admirably then, Clair had thought—albeit a little ridiculously.

He'd motioned them to silence, unwound the damp eider-down from about his shoulders, crept forward, suddenly leaped, landed on top of the deer and proceeded to smother the little animal in the quilt's gaudy folds. Squeals and scuffling. Deer on top, deer underfoot. Sinclair in all directions, but hanging on grimly and cursing so that Clair, running to his aid, had regretted that she'd no note-book with her.

She halted and gasped.

For at her forward rush all the bushes round about, probably held paralyzed by fear until then, had suddenly vomited deer; a good two score of deer. A hoof-clicking like the rattle and an insane orchestra of castanets, the bushes were deserted, and the deer in headlong flight. Clair had stared after them, fascinated, been cursed for her pains, then had knelt down and, rather white-faced, assisted Sinclair to strangle his captive. . . .

Sir John Mullaghan, who had tripped and fallen in his forward rush, had arrived then.

They had kindled a fire and fed on that deer. The making of the fire *had* been a problem until it was discovered that the armaments manufacturer had a petrol-lighter in his pocket. Ornate, gold-mounted thing. No petrol. But the flint had still functioned and there had been lots of dry grass available. Fire in a minute. How to cook the deer? No knives.

Sinclair had said, "Miss Stranlay, go away for a minute. You, Mullaghan, I want your help." Clair had turned away, reluctantly, had heard an unfriendly confabulation, had heard the sound of scuffling, the blow that must have broken the animal's skull, smelled the reek of blood, had wheeled round with a cry. . . . The men had torn a leg and haunch from the body of the deer.

The meal had been good, though singey and tough. Sinclair had burned his fingers in tearing off a half-cooked portion and handing it to her. Sir John, his dress-suit spattered with drops of blood, had helped at the cooking efficiently enough. But there had been no cooperation

between him and Sinclair. They had sat, replete, and disagreed with
each other, never once addressing each other, but talking through the
medium of Clair. It had then been late afternoon.

"It's obvious we must hold inland and southward," said Sinclair.
"There's no sign of human beings or habitations hereabouts. And if
this, as I suspect, is northern Canada in a warm spell, it is only southward we are ever likely to meet with any one."

"I doubt if there's anything in that, Miss Stranlay." The gray head
had been shaken at her; the gentle eyes held determination. "Probably
you, like myself, wish to get back to civilization as soon as possible?
Then, I think we ought to return to the cliff-head before sunset and light
a fire there and wait through the night. Some ship is bound to see the
signal, for there are plenty of ships on the African coast."

Clair wiped her greasy fingers on the coarse grass. "Canada? I don't
think we can be there, Doctor Sinclair. It's too far away from the eastern Atlantic, as Sir John says. But this is not a bit like Africa."

She looked at the three-quarters of deer left to them, and while the
two men looked at her, Sinclair with apparent indifference, Sir John
with courteous attention. "On the other hand, there doesn't seem to be
any food in this place. All those little deer ran away south. They may
have been strays from the south. I think we ought to follow them. After
all, we're bound to meet people some time."

The American had stood up, at that, handed Clair the quilt, seized
the deer, butted it with his hands, and then slung it across the shoulder
of his pajama-jacket. "You've the casting vote. Come on, then."

And they had gone on. They'd camped that night a few miles inland,
under the lee of a ragged and woebegone pine on the edge of the great,
silent forest itself. They had made another fire with the aid of Sir John
Mullaghan's lighter, and broiled more deer and eaten it, all three of
them by then weary and foot-sore from the few miles they'd covered.

WHEN she came back they had apparently settled down for the night.
Sir John was lying down to the left of her. He had removed his
pumps and wrapped his feet with grass. He had also removed his coat
and draped it round his thin shoulders. He lay, close enough to the fire.
It had grown cold, though there was no wind.

Sinclair lay near the fire also, but more directly under the lee of the
pine. He was swathed about by bundles of grass, and Clair had thought,
appalled, "Oh, my good God, I'll have to do some hay-making." But
that had proved unnecessary. Between the spaces occupied by the two
men, and directly opposite the bole of the pine, the quilt had been out-

spread to dry and had dried. This, Clair understood, was her sleeping position. She had sunk into the eider-down gratefully.

"Good night, you two," she had called, muffling the soft folds around about her.

Sinclair had merely grunted.

Sir John had said, uncovering his face, "Good night, Miss Stranlay. Call me if you want anything."

"Tea in the morning, please."

He had laughed, with pleasant courtesy, and there had been silence.

Such silence! All her life she would remember it, though the second night had made it commonplace. The night was a woman, asleep. Sometimes you could hear her breathe. Terrible. And against the sky, unlighted though it was, you saw her hair rise floating now and then. The pine-foliage. . . .

Next day they held south again, with little conversation.

Sinclair had divided up the last leg and haunch for the evening meal. "We don't know when we'll get any other food." The others had assented, Clair silently regretful, for she found herself very hungry in those hours of marching through the clear cold sunshine. Suddenly she had thought, and said aloud with a rush of longing, "Oh, my good God, I do wish I had a cigarette!"

Sir John Mullaghan had come to her aid unexpectedly. "I have two," he had said, and had drawn a small silver case from his pocket the while Clair stared at him unbelievingly. Opened, the case disclosed two veritable Egyptians. Clair had reached for one, starvingly, lighted it from a twig, drawn the acrid sweet smoke down into grateful lungs. Sir John, similarly employed, had sat at the other side of the fire. Sinclair, looking tired, looked into the fire. She had suddenly disliked Mullaghan.

"Share with me, Doctor Sinclair?"

"No, thanks. I don't smoke."

Next morning—the third morning—they had eaten the last of the deer and tramped southward again, across country still unchanged and unchanging in promise. But this morning had greeted them with rain, so that they had been forced to shelter under a great fir, watching the sheets of water warping westward over the long llanos.

"I'm going to hunt around and see if there's any food to be had, Miss Stranlay," Sinclair said.

"I think I'll also look round, Miss Stranlay," Sir John put in immediately.

"There's a fire required," the American had flung over his shoulder curtly. "And Miss Stranlay's tired."

Sir John Mullaghan had searched around for dry grass and twigs, scarce enough commodities, but it was clear that the men were becoming irritable.

Clair wrapped in the quilt, had fallen asleep listening to the slow patter of the rain on the leaves overhead.

Sir John Mullaghan, in a considerably battered dress suit, squatted on bruised and dirty heels, doing futile things with his petrol lighter against a dour loom of treey, desolate landscape. Sinclair had gone hunting and had not yet returned.

They had no method of measuring time, with the sun's face draped in trailing rain-curtains, but it must have been at least another two hours before Sinclair did come back, coming from the direction of the forest, and walking wearily, a soaked and tattered figure.

"You'll catch pneumonia," Clair had called, and tried to stir the fire to warmth-giving. But both she and Sir John had looked at the doctor with sinking hearts. Clair had said, casually, "Any luck?"

Sinclair had opened his right hand. "These."

They were half a dozen half-ripened beechnuts, picked up below a high, solitary and unclimbable tree. Sinclair told, shortly, that he had wandered for miles without sighting any animal or bird or fruit-bearing tree. "And we'd best be getting on again."

"Why?" Clair had queried, eating her two nuts.

"Because you can't stay unsheltered on a night such as this promises to be. We'll try nearer the mountains for some ledge or rock-shelter."

So once again they had set out southward, with the rain presently clearing merely to display a sun hovering on the verge of setting.

A ND now, in the last of the daylight, lost, desperate and foolish, they stood on the brink of a disastrous quarrel, Sinclair with every appearance of being about to assault the armaments manufacturer, Sir John with his gentle face ablaze. Clair looked from one to the other of them, wanly, but still with that gay irony that was her salvation, and, after a little calculation, did the thing that she thought would be best.

She burst into tears.

The two men paused. The American, she observed through her fingers, went more haggard than ever. Sir John laid his hand on her arm.

"Miss Stranlay, you must keep up. We can't be far now from some town or village or a trapper's hut."

"You're spoiling all our chances because you won't act together."

There was a silence. Sinclair looked at the volcanoes, looked at Clair. "That's true, Miss Stranlay . . . I'm sorry, Mullaghan."

"And I, Doctor Sinclair."

The American turned again and led them onward.

Suddenly they found themselves in the lee of one of the foot-hills, under the mouths of two great caves.

CHAPTER FOUR—*The Lair*

"WE DON'T know what may be in them," said Sir John Mullaghan. They stood and looked at the cave-mouths. Hesitating, they peered at one another. A little stream of water, hardly seen, ran coldly over Clair's toes.

"What can there be? There are no animals in this country. Do let's get out of the rain—it's coming on again."

"Can't you smell?" said Sinclair.

Clair elevated her small rain-beaded nose and smelled. A faint yet acrid odor impinged on the rainy evening. Ammoniac. "Like the Zoo lion-house," said Sinclair, very low, staring at the near cave-mouth.

The armaments manufacturer showed his latent quality. He bent down, groped at his feet and straightened with a large stone in his hand. He motioned them aside. Clair stood still. Sinclair seized her roughly by the shoulder and pulled her to one side of the near cave-mouth.

"Come out!"

The stone crashed remotely in the bowels of the cave, ricochetted in darkness, stirred a multitude of echoes. Nothing else. The twilight vanished. They stood in the soft sweep of the rain, listening.

"I'll step into the mouth and try my lighter on a bit of my under-clothes," said Sir John practically.

"All right." The American's voice imperturbable.

Clair could see neither of them now. But Sinclair's shoulder touched hers. She heard cautious, barefoot treadings in the dark. Sir John had left them. Clair thought, 'Oh, God, why doesn't he hurry?'

The forward darkness spat sparks intermittently. The lighter. *Spat. Spat.* Something dirty white. A catch. Vigorous blowing. A glow. The mouth of the cave. Porous-looking rock. Mullaghan's face. His voice.

"It winds inward. I'll go and see if there's anything."

"All right."

Clair said, "No, you don't. Doctor Sinclair thinks he's protecting me. I don't need it." She prodded her protector. "Go with him."

His support was withdrawn. "Keep where you are."

A faint glow, over-gloomed by a titanic shadow, illumined the cave-mouth. Between her and that glow passed another tenebrous Titan.

The glow failed, lighted up again, receded. Alone. Soft swish of rain.
Clair began to count, found herself swaying, shook herself out of count-
ing. "Makes you sleepy." A long wait and then suddenly Sinclair's voice
close at hand, "Miss Stranlay!"

"Hello?"

"Give me your hand." She found herself drawn forward. "Careful."

"Nothing inside?"

"Not a thing except a queer kind of nest."

She stumbled in blackness. "Has the light gone out?"

"The cave twists."

The ground underfoot had a porous feeling: it was as though one
walked over the surface of a frozen sponge. A few more steps and
Sinclair guided Clair round a corner of the ante-cave. She saw then a
roof nine or ten feet high overarching a cave-chamber something of the
size and appearance of her own small drawing-room in Kensington. It
glittered grayly. On the uneven floor, tending a small fire that seemed to
be fed with his undergarments and a pile of ancient hay, squatted Sir
John Mullaghan, naked to the waist. In the far leftward corner was a
hummock. The "nest."

"All right, Miss Stranlay?"

"As rain, Sir John." Clair stumbled again. Sinclair pushed her past
the fire. She sank down on the nest. Its straw crackled dustily under
her weight. The fire, Sir John, and Sinclair began to pace a hasting
gavotte. Clair closed her eyes.

"I'm going to faint."

SHE passed from the faint into a sleep, and awoke several hours later,
Sinclair's hand shaking her.

"Miss Stranlay . . . I'm afraid it's going to spring—"

She sat up with twinging body, brushing back the hair from her
face. The American crouched beside her, a red-ochered shadow in the
light of the fire, his head turned toward the fire. The fire itself burned
and sputtered sulkily under a strange, brittle heaping of fuel. And beyond its light, in the darkness, glowed another light.

Two of them. Unwinking. Clair felt an acid saliva collect in her
mouth. Suddenly the two lights changed position: they had sunk lower
toward the floor of the cave. Clair understood. It was crouching.

"Don't scream."

Sinclair's words were in a whisper. But the Thing in the darkness beyond the fire must have heard them. Its eyes reared up again. Clair shut
her own; opened them. The eyes were again sinking. Spring this time?

And then the fire took a hand. It spiraled upward a long trail of smoke, red-glowing gas which burst into crackling flame. There came a violent sneeze, a snarl, the thump of a heavy body crashing against the side of the cave in a backward leap. And then the three survivors of the *Magellan's Cloud* saw—saw for a moment a bunched, barred, gigantic body, a coughing, snarling, malignant face. Then a rushing patter filled the cave. The fire died down. Beyond its light no eyes now glowed in the darkness.

Clair sank on her elbow. "What was it?"

Some one beyond Sinclair drew a long breath. "A tiger."

Sinclair spoke very quietly. "Like one, but it wasn't."

"What was it, then?" Clair saw Sir John Mullaghan also crouching, a keyed-up shadow.

The American, answering, still stared across the fire. *"Machærodus."*

"What?"

"Machærodus—a saber-toothed tiger."

There fell a moment's silence—of stupefaction on the part of all three. Clair, ill, closed her eyes and opened them again. She must be dreaming. "But—it can't be. They're extinct."

"Didn't you see the tusks?"

She had. So had Sir John. The latter got to his feet.

"It may come back."

The fire purred and crackled again. He had fed it from a pile of fuel not in the cave when they first entered it. The American got up and helped him. Clair's head, sleep-weighted, sank again on the nest. She thought, "I'm dreaming. Don't care though it's a mammoth next time." The smell of the fuel was nauseating. She voiced a sleepy question, and, voicing it, was asleep, and never heard Sinclair's answer.

"What are you burning?"

"Bones."

WHEN next she awoke, she was in complete darkness. No fire burned near at hand. She had a sense of having slept for many hours. She stretched, cautiously, remembering everything. A keen cool current of air blew steadily in her face.

If that three-day Odyssey across the deserted savanna was a dream? . . . She was at home in Kensington. . . . Wrapped in a quilt, lying in fusty hay? She called cautiously: "Doctor Sinclair!"

No answer. She released her left arm, and sought in the place where he had crouched while they looked at the Eyes beyond the fire. Her fingers touched bare rock. She sat up, frightened, desperately hungry.

"Doctor Sinclair!"

A far-off voice called, "Coming, Miss Stranlay."

Footsteps, and the darkness receding from the light of a smoky torch, held in Sinclair's hand. In his other he carried a shapeless bundle.

She said, "Goodness, nice to see you. Where's the fire? Have I slept long?"

"The fire's in the outer half of the cave. It's about noon."

"You *are* a dear—though you try so desperately not to be."

The dear grunted.

Clair's eyes twinkled at him. "Is that a smell of something cooking?"

"We've found some food."

She had remembered the beast that had stalked them in the dark hours. Had there been any beast? She snatched up the torch and walked past the ashes of the fire. On the damp floor were multitudes of impressions and superimposed on these great pug-marks of a big cat.

She picked up the eider-down quilt and groped her way through to the front part of the cave, and so came in sight of it suddenly, the entrance flooded with sunlight, and against that sunlight a hazy drift of smoke, as from the lips of a contemplative smoker, engendered by the fire. Either side of this fire sat Sinclair and Sir John—Sinclair in his ragged pajamas, Sir John with his slight form even slighter than of yore.

The faces of both men were lined with stubble, an unchancy harvest, Sir John's a red wiriness of vegetal promise, with hints of gray, Sinclair's a blue-black down. Their hair stood up in tufts and feathers. But both of them seemed to have washed.

"Morning, Sir John. I've already met you, Doctor. . . . Oh, not in the wilds." She motioned them to sit. . . . "Where did you get the food?"

Sir John was toasting on a sliver of wood a strange-looking, yellowish piece of meat. Sinclair bent his dark poll over a roundish, smooth-polished object. Sir John seemed to hesitate a second in his reply.

"Doctor Sinclair found it, Miss Stranlay. We've already eaten some, but you slept too soundly to be awakened. Better now?"

"Yes, much." She stared at Sir John's preparations. *"Found it?"*

The American glanced up impatiently. "Nothing mysterious. It won't poison you—I saw to that. It's horse-flesh. There was a partly eaten carcass about a hundred yards from the mouth of the cave here."

"Oh! So I didn't dream last night. There was a beast like a tiger prowling on the other side of the fire?"

The armaments manufacturer held up the skewer of yellowish meat, looking the most incongruous of cooks as he did so. "Yes. Some kind of tiger. It probably killed the pony after it ceased to stalk us." Clair regarded her breakfast uncertainly.

"I think I'll wash first. Both of you have. Where?"

"Just outside the cave, to the left."

Clair went out. Sinclair looked at Sir John, said something. The armaments manufacturer rose up and followed Clair.

"I'm sorry, Miss Stranlay, but one of us had better be near. That beast may come back, though it's not very likely."

"I see." Clair felt and sounded ungracious—and, as usual, regretted it. She looked away, across the tundra flowering into swamp, at the sun-hazed surface of the mile-distant forest, and then southward, where swamp and forest crept down to the foot-hills, and their long journey through the llanos-land seemed to end. What was beyond that cul-de-sac? . . . She became aware of Sir John waiting. "Sorry. Shan't keep you a minute. Do wish I had some soap."

"There's red earth on the bank here. I used it. It seemed fairly effective."

HE SIGHED and turned his head away from her. The sun seemed warmer. A little breeze stirred the long grass. The stream glimmered and its gurgling passage was the only sound to be heard. And the same thought came to him as to Clair: What lay south?

He became aware of Clair standing beside him, dabbing at her face and hands with a bunch of grass. "That was good . . . Sir John."

He looked gently into her grave eyes.

"*What* country is this? It can't be Canada. And it can't be Africa."

He shook his head. "I'm afraid I haven't an opinion worth knowing, Miss Stranlay. Tigers, I think, are found in the East Indies. But to suppose the *Magellan's Cloud* drifted across the Atlantic, America and the Pacific in those few hours four nights ago is absurd. And I can not imagine this stretch of uninhabited country in the East Indies."

Clair finished dabbing, retied the fraying neck-loop of her jacket. "No. But we must be getting near some inhabited place."

"I hope so."

The American stood in the sunlight at the mouth of the second cave, joined them. His usually dour face was alive with some strayed excitement.

"Feel hungry?" he asked her.

"Shockingly." But indeed her appetite felt oddly reserved. She sat down beside the fire, but still in the sunlight. She picked up the piece of charred horseflesh and began to eat it.

"How did you manage to cut it up?"

"With this." Sinclair was back at the other side of the fire. He held up an object. Clair peered at it. Passed it to her. She turned it over, wonderingly.

It was a fragment of stone, she thought, though it was flint. Even to her unaccustomed eyes it seemed to have a certain artificiality.

It was in the form of a smooth-butted ax-blade—an incredibly crude stone ax-blade.

"Why—it's *made*."

The American nodded. "It's *made*."

"Where did you find it?"

"In the next case. Among a pile of bones."

She remembered something. She questioned him with her eyes. He nodded.

"Human bones. Though I didn't know that in the darkness last night when I was searching for fuel. Fortunately I didn't burn them all."

She looked at the thing at his feet, and somehow didn't want any more of the horse-flesh. It was a skull he had been examining. She stood up and went to the entrance. Sir John glanced at her. Something like a smile of sympathy flickered over his face.

The American said abruptly: "You people."

They both turned. Sinclair had the skull in his hands. He came toward them. The stone ax-blade slipped out of Clair's forgetful hand as she backed away from the skull. Sinclair sprang forward and caught it, bruising his fingers. He swore. Sir John turned his head; Clair tried hard to repress herself, failed; giggled. Sir John's laughter joined with hers.

"I'm sorry." Genuinely contrite.

"All right. I want to talk to you both about these finds." He addressed Sir John, still with something of an effort. "Know anything about crania?"

Sir John shook his head. "Nothing at all." He took the skull in his hand, however, and examined it. It was complete to jaw-bone and teeth. He held it out to Clair. She waved it away.

"No thanks. Ghastly thing. It's got a permanent frown, too."

Sinclair: "Exactly. That's the point. It's not an ordinary skull."

"A savage's?" said Clair helpfully.

"Of course it's a savage's. Otherwise he wouldn't have had a flint hand-ax in his possession when he was carried back in there and devoured by the saber-tooth."

Clair shivered. "Was that what happened?" She looked over the undulating waste of grass to the dark holes of the forest. "Ugh!"

Sir John glanced at her, and interposed gently: "And what is peculiar about the skull?"

"It's as Miss Stranlay says. It has a permanent frown—look, this ridge above the eyes. And practically no forehead. Look at the teeth."

They looked. "Funny," said Clair, at once repulsed and fascinated. Sinclair closed the jaw again, set the skull at his feet, stared at it.

"Not a human skull at all, you know, as we understand the term human. By rights it belongs to a race that died off twenty thousand years ago."

Clair was startled into dim memories of casual reading in prehistory. "What race?"

"The Neanderthal. It's a Neanderthal skull."

B Y EARLY afternoon they had left the caves some four or five miles behind, and, tramping along the edge of the foothills, were nearing the spot where hills and forest converged. Sinclair, as usual, walked in advance. He was burdened with the remains of the horse-flesh, a great haunch, and the cord of his pajamas sagged under the weight of the flint ax-head. The strange skull he had abandoned.

Clair and Sir John walked side by side, half a dozen yards behind him. Sir John said, "I'm afraid we're rather a drag on our leader. By the way, have you noticed how much alike your names are—Clair and Sinclair?"

She looked after the long-striding figure of the American, and unconsciously increased her own pace. "He's the saint and I'm the Clair. . . . I'm sure that's why they used to martyr saints. What did you think of the skull?"

"I don't know what to think. Though I should imagine that the chances are Doctor Sinclair has made a mistake."

"Neanderthal man. . . . They all died off in the last Glacial Age—I think. Or was it just after it? Perhaps it was a fossil skull."

The armaments manufacturer, striding barefoot, bow-shouldered beside her, shook his head. "No, it wasn't that. I'm afraid I know little or nothing of such matters, but it was comparatively fresh bone."

They were at a slight elevation by then. The forest did not close completely on the hills, but left a narrow corridor, a waste, bush-strewn space. Across this space they looked, and it was as if they were at no slight elevation, but on a mountain-side. For beyond the passageway the land failed completely, as it seemed.

Yet, remote and far away, downward, southward, something like a lake shimmered, forest-fringed; and, blue and golden, there shone under the sunlight a suggestion of immense tracts of waste country. All three of the travelers stared, Clair with sinking heart. It must be miles to that lake. And no sign anywhere of a native village or trading station.

"We're on a high level—a plateau with mountains," said Sinclair unemotionally. "We've been traveling across it for days. That's why we've seen few animals. There's nothing here but strays from down there."

Sir John said, "And we're going down?"

"Yes."

Clair smiled at the American, casually, friendlily. "There's no 'yes' about it. Not until we've all made up our minds."

Sinclair's ears tinted themselves a slow red. "*I* am going down."

"Do."

Sir John interposed. "Really, Miss Stranlay, I don't think there is anything else to be done now. . . . Though possibly Doctor Sinclair might word his invitations a little more courteously in the future."

Sinclair scowled at him angrily. "Courtesy! Do you realize we're absolutely lost somewhere in absolutely unknown and unexplored country? That there are *machærodi* and possibly other wild beasts in it—to say nothing of Neanderthalers?"

"That seems to be the case," said Clair. "But it doesn't alter the fact that your manners are badly in need of improvement."

He glanced from one to the other of them, as though he were looking at idiots. He shrugged. "All right. Bad though they may be, I think it would be ruinous if we split into two parties." He bowed, a ludicrous angry figure. "Would you mind coming down into the low country, Miss Stranlay?"

Clair had a ridiculous impulse. They stared at her startled as she sang and held out her arms to the wild lands below them:

> "Oh, ye'll take the high road,
> And I'll take the low road,
> And I'll be in Scotland afore ye;
> But me and my true love,
> We'll never meet again
> On the bonny, bonny banks of Loch Lomond!"

Sir John said gently, "Thank you, Miss Stranlay."

"Silly," Clair confessed.

"Not silly at all, Miss Stranlay." It was Sinclair unexpectedly. "Thank you also. I was a lout."

IT WAS a steeply shelving descent of nearly a mile, over the usual coarse grass. At the foot Sinclair waited—as usual. He avoided Clair's eyes. "We have about an hour until sunset."

Sir John, panting, sat down. "And what are we going to do until then?"

The American seemed for once at a loss. "Find a place to camp, I suppose."

"Looks different somehow," said Clair.

It did. The forest was more widely spread or the tundra more enforested, according to one's fancy. Some oaks—young-looking oaks—grew near at hand. Smooth hog-backed hills rose here and there in the tree-set waste, but there were no mountains, no volcanoes. Also, near sunset though it was, this low country was much warmer than the plateau they had just deserted. Nor was it so silent.

A long-necked gray bird flitted among the oaks; they could hear the swish of its wings through the leaves. Remote among the low smooth-humped hills a vast long-drawn moan rose and fell; they had not noticed it at first, because it was part of the landscape. Now, as it ceased, they peered in the direction from which it had come.

"A cow," said Clair.

It did indeed sound like the lowing of a cow—a gigantic cow. Presently it ceased with some decision, and was not resumed. Sinclair stood with his fingers on his hand-ax. "Bison, perhaps."

"What *is* this place, Doctor Sinclair?"

"Eh? . . . God knows."

"I doubt it," said Clair.

The American began to move across the grass toward the trees. Clair held out her hand to Sir John, but he stood up without assistance, albeit with a grimace. Presently they were threading a new belt of trees, very green and lush with undergrowth, and with their shadows pointing long dark fingers into the west. The gray bird was silent. So was all else of the hidden life of the tree-spaces—if there were life. Clair heard herself in a whisper: "Where are we going?"

Sinclair's voice also was low. "Some place where there's water."

They emerged from the trees then, into another clearing. Doing so, Clair seemed to hear a sound of low rumblings, like the borborygmus in a large and placid stomach. She thought rather ruefully, "Not mine." And went on, following the sunset-reddened back of Sinclair. Neither he nor Sir John had heard anything.

But suddenly they did. Fallen boughs crunched and snapped, and something with a heavy tread came after them from the twilight darkness of the trees.

They all halted, looking back. For a moment they could distinguish nothing, though the heavy tread paced toward them. And then they saw it against the dun light of an open patch—its swaying bulk, its matted shagginess. Its trunk was lowered, sniffing the track they had taken.

They stared appalled. They had all seen its like before—in this or that museum or illustration. There could be no mistaking those curved immensities of tusk.

It was a mammoth.

CHAPTER FIVE—"And I'll take the low road"

THEY camped a quarter of an hour or so later, by the mere of the lake that had glittered its invitation from the northern plateau. Tall reeds grew far out into the water, and, remotely over that water, unknown birds croaked and dipped amid long grasses that Sinclair certified were—of all things—wild wheat. The American knelt under the moss-shaggy boughs of a great oak, coaxing Sir John's lighter to embed a spark in a tuft of withered grass. Sunset was again close—the lingering sunset of a temperate country. It might have been eight in the evening.

Clair padded to and fro, bough-collecting, with her bare feet just a little chilled by the evening dew. Sir John, outside the obscuring bulk of the oak, was looking back to the dimness of the plateau brow.

And the mammoth continued to watch them.

It was halted at a distance of ten yards or so, not facing them, but in profile. Its great ears flapped meditatively and every now and then its trunk would stray upward into the foliage of a bush, or down into the unappetizing grass. The sunset glimmered on its watching eye. . . .

It had trailed them like a great retriever, halting when they halted, coming on again as they moved hesitatingly away. While they crossed a clear space it would stop and watch them, pawing a little, rubbing a gigantic hair-fringed shoulder against a tree. Then it would pace swingingly after them. Once, apparently imagining them lost, it had frolicked wildly amid the bushes, hunting the scent of them with uplifted trunk.

"It must be harmless," Clair had whispered.

"Trying to summon up courage to charge," hazarded Sinclair.

"Hope it comes of a timid family."

"I'm afraid we can't do anything to prevent it charging, anyhow," said Sir John, glancing over his shoulder and starting a little. ". . . I thought it was coming that time."

But it had not, and, the lake opening out before them, there had been no other course obvious than to camp. It was eery doing so with that watching monster pretending not to watch them. Clair knelt by Sinclair with a handful of twigs seeing he had caught a spark and was cherishing the grass into the parturition of a flame.

He glanced at her. "The fire may scare it off or may madden it into making an attack. Scoot round the back of the tree if it comes." He spoke in a whisper. "Frightened?"

Clair fed the flame with a twig, resolutely keeping her eyes from the watcher. "Not now. Rather a thrill. . . . What's it doing now?"

Sir John came to their side. "I think it's going to charge."

The mammoth had knelt on its knees, embedding its immense tusks in a great clump of grass. There came a crackling, tearing sound. The mammoth stood up. Its tusks were laden with grass, like the rake of a hay-maker. Elevating its trunk to the fodder, it proceeded to test and devour great wisps.

"Bless it," said Clair, "it's having its supper."

The armaments manufacturer ruffled his gray hair. "One certainly didn't expect such mildness. A *mammoth!*"

There the brute stood, real enough, feeding and watching them, with the brown night closing down behind him. The flame came now in little spurts and glows and the twigs caught; cautiously, Sinclair administered first small branches, then larger ones. The firelight went out across the gloaming shadows, splashing gently on the red-brown coat and bare, creased skull of the mammoth. It paused for a little in its eating, turning its trunk toward them. Then resumed. Clair sat down.

"A mammoth in the twentieth century! It's—oh, it's ridiculous."

Sir John, standing and looking at the watcher, patted her shoulder. Sinclair hacked at the dried horse-meat with the Neanderthal ax. The meat had a faint smell of decay. He said, "I've been thinking about where we are. I know now it can't be Canada."

"And it certainly is not Africa, as I thought," murmured Sir John.

"No. I think we're in Patagonia."

CLAIR drew back warmed toes from the fire. Abruptly the last of the daylight went. The lake misted from a pale sheen to a dark, rippling mystery. The sound of the mammoth feeding was oddly homelike. . . .

"But I understand practically all of it has been explored," said Sir John.

Sinclair toasted yellow meat for a moment. "I don't think so. Delusion we North Americans and English have about every country which is shown plainly on a map, with the main mountains and rivers."

He stopped and frowned at the piece of meat. He addressed Clair. He still avoided, as far as possible, speaking directly to Sir John.

"Did you notice from the plateau brow the mere tips of a mountain range—they must be more than fifty miles away—down there in the south, Miss Stranlay?"

Clair nodded.

"I think they must be the Andes. We're somewhere in the western Argentine or the foot-hills of Chili—the country where Pritchard went to hunt the great sloth. We may be traversing a mountain kink or fold that up to this time has completely escaped notice."

Clair thought. Then: "A kink with saber-toothed tigers and fresh Neanderthal skulls in it—and also mammoths?"

"All possible." But his voice sounded less certain.

Sir John said: "But not very probable. We landed on a seacoast somewhere, went inland and turned south. That seacoast, if this is South America, must have been the Atlantic. And Patagonia, if my memory serves me, is remote from the Atlantic. Also, it has grown warmer the farther south we have come. If we are south of the equator it ought to grow colder."

Sinclair detached the piece of meat from its wooden skewer and handed it to Clair. He nodded acknowledgment of Sir John's arguments and was silent. All three of them sat and ate the tough meat. Then, stumbling among the reeds, they went down to the lake in search of water. At a spot that glimmered faintly Sinclair lay down full length and drank. Sir John followed suit. Clair squatted and cupped the water in her hands and drank that way. As they came back to the fire they noted the mammoth still in guardianship.

Sir John raked about in the shadows outside the fire, collecting damp grass and arranging it for drying to act as pillows and mattresses. Clair sat a yard or so from Sinclair, looking into the fire, drowsy and still a little hungry after her meager ration of horseflesh. Sinclair had procured a long bough and was whittling at it doggedly with the flint-ax.

"Stone Age idyl," murmured Clair.

"Eh?"

She repeated the words, and, as she did so, remote away beyond the lake, strange and eery, that lowing they had heard in the early afternoon broke out again. It rose and belled and fell, the calling of some stray of a Titan herd.

Unexpectedly, for he had been quiet enough until then, the mammoth answered, lifting his trunk in the remote washings of the firelight and trumpeting screamingly.

Clair thought her ear-drums would burst. She covered them and heard the noise die down. The ensuing quietness held no hint of distant lowing.

But to Clair, with it dead, there came an almost passionate wish that it would break out again. She looked at the two men, at the darkness around them, at the bulk of the strange beast that guarded them so queerly. That lowing and wild trumpeting seemed to have torn down a barrier inside her heart—that calling across wild spaces heard in the shelter of the camp-fire. . . . She had heard it before, somewhere, at some time, in an era that knew not print and publishers. Often.

"Miss Stranlay!" Sir John's hand on her shoulder. "You'd best lie down if you're so sleepy. You nearly fell into the fire."

"DID I?"

She shook herself and looked at them. Sinclair, hafting his ax-head on the bough and binding it with sinews he had saved from the tiger-killed pony, had half-risen to catch her just as Sir John forestalled him. He sank down again. The armaments manufacturer, padding about barefoot, arranged the grass beds. He looked over at Clair, hearing her low laugh.

"Nothing much, Sir John. But I'd just said to Doctor Sinclair, before that trumpeting started, that this was a Stone Age idyl. And just now I caught sight of your clothes."

The firelight twinkled on a gray head and the smile on a gentle cultured face. "And they don't fit the part?"

The American laughed shortly. "The warrior was the armaments manufacturer of the Stone Age, Miss Stranlay, and no doubt wore appropriate habiliments."

Clair felt a little pang of shame for him. The fire simmered cheerfully. Sir John straightened and looked across at the deportee.

"Yes, the warrior was probably the equivalent of the armaments manufacturer," he said quietly. "He brought order and a livable relationship into primitive anarchy. And his task isn't yet finished."

Clair said: "Perhaps it hasn't begun in this country yet. . . . Funniest nightmare of a country we've landed in! I'd give anything for clothes and a bathroom, an electric light and—oh, for a cigarette!"

She paused and tried to put into unfacile words that strange aching that had been in her heart on hearing the lowing in the distant hills.

"But there's something in it that's not terrifying at all. Lovely, rather. The silence and starkness. . . . Those primitives of the Old Stone Age—they had some elemental contacts with beauty that we've lost forever."

Sir John Mullaghan sat clasping his knees, rubbing his chilled bare feet. He shook his head. "They had this kind of country, perhaps, but it was not the country you see with your civilized, romantic eyes, Miss Stranlay. It was a waste for ghouls for them. The night was a horror to the squatting-places—the time when the dead Old Men of the tribes returned as stalking carnivora, the time of shuddering fear.

"It was a life livable only for the strongest and most brutal. For thousands and thousands of years life was that only. And here and there rose the soldier and the inventor, the men who subjected the squalid and lowly, who built the first classes and sowed the first seeds. And the long climb from filth and futility began."

"Poor ancestors!" Clair said it soberly, her eyes on the night.

Sinclair finished binding his ax, and laid it on his knees and looked into the fire.

"That was the life of the Stone Age savage, Miss Stranlay. And the strong men and the wise men, and the warriors and the witch-doctors, bound him in chains of taboo—the first laws—and made him less of a beast. For twenty thousand years they've fashioned new chains for him, till civilized man has taken the place of the savage. But it's been no simple case of design.

"The old, meaningless taboos and loyalties—once necessary and just —are things that threaten to strangle us nowadays. The age of the witch-doctors and the warrior is over. But they won't believe it. They still preach their obscene gods and raise and equip armies that now threaten to smash to atoms the foundations of civilization. It is they who are the ghouls who haunt the contemporary world."

Sir John said steadily: "They are the ghouls, if you like, that guard civilization. The strong man keeps his house and the wise country an army on the *qui vive*. The soldier is civilization's safeguard, and still, thank God, defends it against anarchic sentimentalists. . . . Do you people know nothing of the beast that is in human nature unless there is force and discipline to keep it down? I had a daughter once. Twelve years of age. Bright and clean and very glad to be alive. . . . She was missing one night. She was found under some bushes a mile or so away from home next day. She had been murdered by a tramp."

Clair made an inarticulate sound of sympathy. Sinclair's knuckles whitened round his ax-haft. "I have seen humans murdered and mutilated in thousands. And through no chance accident of madness. Sentimentalist? My good God, you old men! Sentimentalists we are then, and our fight is for human sanity. Don't think we shirk facts. And we've learned from experience.

"We know that man's a fighting animal by nature, that cruelty's his birth-right; and we also know that what keeps us in the pit as animals are the armies and the armaments. We're out to smash both, we who have had some personal experience of both."

Clair's voice startled them. "I had a fiancé in 1917. A boy. He'd have hated to hurt the hatefullest human on earth. He went to France because I taunted him. He died on the barb-wire at Mametz. All night. He screamed my name all night. . . . And at heart he was just a savage filled with lust and cruelty?"

They said nothing, uncomfortably.

She leaned back with her hands under her head. They had all three forgotten the mammoth. Now they heard its steady munching. Clair thought, with a reckless change to gaiety, "It'll have tummy-ache if it's not careful." She said, "There come the stars. We're hopelessly lost, but they're still the same as ever."

IN THE morning the mammoth was gone. There was no trace of it but the trampled stretch of grass and a great heap of dung. Wakening the first of the three, Clair thought she heard remote trumpetings. But whether these were memories from night-time dreams, or the farewell callings of their mysterious guardian, there was nothing now in the quietude of the morning to tell her.

The fire was a gray fluff. They had slept beyond the first chill of the dawn, and the sunshine in the grays and green of England, sprayed through the lattice-patterns of the oak boughs.

Sinclair slept near Clair with his arms outflung and begrimed, his bearded face hid in his shoulder. Clair reached and touched that shoulder with the tips of her fingers, found it cold, pulled the eider-down quilt over it, and stood up.

Sir John Mullaghan slept huddled in his stained coat, his gray-streaked hair ruffled every now and then by a stray waft of wind.

Clair wondered if she should make a fire. But either Sinclair or Sir John had the lighter. She moved about under the oak, and farther into the bushes, collecting twigs. She found a stretch of gorse-bushes, very yellow and scented, still wet with the night-mist. It was as she stood among them that the lark began to sing.

It was at first no more than a remote piping up in the gray pearlment of the sky. But it came nearer, and the sound hovered, and shading her eyes, it seemed to Clair that she saw the fluttering singer for a moment. She stood and listened and found herself weeping.

It died away. Clair picked up the firewood and went back to the camping place. The men still slept. For a little she considered them and then went down through the dark, seeping peat-edges to the mere of the lake. A bird flew out of the reeds as she approached. A kingfisher. From her feet the cold of the ground spread up through her body.

She undressed, a simple matter, and waded out, into a clamoring pain of coldness. Her hair fell over her face and she switched her mind to that matter as the water rose higher, over her knees, creeping upward. . . . "Getting long, and where will you find a barber's shop? Unless Sinclair operates with his flint-ax. . . . Now? Deep enough?"' She halted, halfknelt, and then flung herself forward.

Deep enough.

She swam into the sunrise through a long lane in the reeds. Beyond that lane, cramp caught her right arm for a moment and she struggled with it, a little frightened, until it passed. The lake swept to the horizon almost, she saw, though from its surface there was no sign of Sinclair's Andes. . . . Alligators?

But there seemed nothing living in the region of the lake, apart from the skimming kingfishers. She turned round at last and swam toward the remote solitary oak. As she did so she suffered from the curious illusion that it waved to and fro, violently, as in a high wind. A thin pencil-point of smoke was rising. It did the same.

"Curious. Something wrong with your heart?"

Soberly, she reached the shore and dressed, and went through the reeds, hearing the anxious calling of Sinclair and Sir John, whom an earthquake of considerable intensity had disturbed in the preparation of breakfast.

CLAIR thought: "We are in the Hollow Land."
   There were high hills both to right and left now as they pressed south. For four or five miles they kept to the bank of the lake, but that was soon left behind, a radiance that presently betook itself from the earth to the sky. The leftward hills were the farther away, and between them rose and fell in long undulations a crazy scraping of nullahs. Underfoot was the long grass, but of finer texture here than on the northward plateau, growing in places lush and emerald.

It was a land of streams. They forded three—one at a trampled place, where were the imprints of both tiny hoofs and great paws.

"Why are we still going south?" Clair asked once.

"Because we might as well," the American returned broodingly.

Sir John suffered from agonies of stomach-aches throughout that day. He walked beside Clair with distorted face and frequently distorted body. Several times he sat down while the other two stood and waited. Sinclair could do nothing for him—or at least offered to do nothing. Neither he nor Clair had as yet been affected by the saltless diet of horseflesh.

Sinclair carried his ax-blade hafted now on a five-foot pole. He stalked a sound in the bushes with it once, only to disturb a long tawny shape which snarled at him sleepily. Then it turned and slunk unhurriedly into deeper cover. Sinclair, rather pale, rejoined the other two.

"What was it?" Clair asked.

He glanced at Sir John. "A lion."

They went on. Once, far toward the leftward hills, and beyond the nullahs, they heard that lowing break out again. Several times herds of small deer were observable at a distance.

Clair looked at them carnivorously. But the wind went steadily south and at the first whiff of the travelers, the deer had gone.

"How many more meals?" Clair asked the American, looking without appetite at the shrinking haunch of horse-flesh. Sinclair had dropped back from his old position in the van and walked beside the other two now.

"Two, I think."

Sir John, padding along in pain, grimaced. "You may count it three. I—I don't think I'll be hungry for some time."

"Oh, the doctor may be able to stalk something fresh," said Clair.

Instead, it was something fresh that presently stalked them, though they never caught sight of it. The noise of its padding pursuit and appraisal began to the right of a long corridor of bushes. The three went on for a little while, and then halted, listening. The stalker had halted also. In the sunshine silence, they heard the noise of its heavy breathing. And a sound of a *swish-swish* among the leaves. ("It's tail,") thought Clair. Sinclair changed from the left-hand side of the march to the right. They waited. No movement of approach. They went forward.

The paddings and cracklings came after them, till beyond the bushes they were in open grassland again and the stalker gave them up.

At noon they made a fire near the usual stream, and Sinclair toasted the meat. Sir John lay full length on the ground, his face hidden, saying nothing. Clair, who had been looking about her as they trekked, walked a quarter of a mile or so away across the Llano, into a patch of gorse-like bushes. Presently she emerged from these coming back with her hands held like a cup.

As she came near the fire she called, "Sir John!"

He looked up at her and smiled wryly, his face drawn with pain.

She knelt beside him. Her hands were filled with blueberries.

"Now you can lunch."

"You are a very sweet lady."

Sinclair said, evenly: "You shouldn't eat too many of them, else it'll be as bad for you as the meat. Some horse, Miss Stranlay?"

They went on again, after Clair had fallen asleep and slept a dream-filled hour in the sun. The southward nullah-jumble drew nearer with its background of hills.

In mid-afternoon they came upon the giant deer.

It stood with head lowered, drinking at a pool, with dark-brown back pelt and white-dappled belly. It was quite close to them when they came through a belt of trees on it, and it was a moment before Clair realized its hugeness. Then she saw Sinclair's six feet two in outline against the thing: it had the bulk of a small elephant.

From its head uprose a twelve-foot spread of antlers, velvet-rimmed. Clair thought, "They must weigh half a ton." The brute slowly lifted its head and regarded them with vague indifferent eyes. Then it inhaled deeply, coughed and trotted away, unhurryingly, westward. They stared after it, seeing it clear the dip of a nullah in one magnificent bound, and then disappear through a pass in the hills.

And presently over those hills came the hunters.

THEY came like figures on a Grecian frieze upflung against the colors of the sunset.

First, there was the afternoon quietness but for the scuffle of the grass underfoot. The sun overhung the hills, the country lay deserted since the great deer had vanished. Clair had bent to pick a thorn from her foot and her companions also had halted, Sir John lifting his face, smelling at some unusual odor he imagined upon the wind. Then—

The first intimation was a far wild neighing and stamping. Clair straightened and looked at the other two. Their eyes were on the grass-covered hilltop perhaps a quarter of a mile away. Its rim was set with hasting dots—dots that changed, enlarged, to wild ponies in panic flight.

The drumming of their hoofs came down to the watchers. Up over the hill into full view they thundered, with flowing manes and tails, thundering against the sunset. And behind company on company, racing into view, came the hunters.

They ran in silence, tall and naked, the sunshine glistening on golden bodies, their hair flying like the horses' manes. Golden and wonderful against the hillcrest they ran, and the staring Sinclair drew a long breath.

"Good God, they are running as fast as the horses!"

It was unbelievable. It was true. And while Sinclair and Sir John stared at now one hunter, now another, overtake his prey and spear it with whirling weapon, Clair Stranlay put her hands in her lips and whistled up through the evening that piercing blast learned long before in the streets of Battersea.

CHAPTER SIX—A Slip in the Time-Spirals

THOSE ensuing moments! Looking back on them Clair was to wonder, with a strange tautness of her heart-strings, if they were indeed as her memory pictured them. If the fervor of the sunset behind the hunters had indeed been so intense, their approach to the three survivors of the *Magellan* so rapid.

They had come fleeting down the hill, a wash of gold, with the speed of converging clouds in a rain-storm. Abandoning the carcasses of the ponies they had swooped downward in a bright torrent, and in Clair's memory she had fast-closed her eyes at sight of their spears. She had thought:

"They will throw those spears."

But they had not. She had opened her eyes again, to find that Sinclair, upright with scowling face, had moved a little in front of her, as though to shield her from the approaching savages. Close now.

And then indeed in her heart had leaped that strange quiver of unreality upon which her memory insisted—or was that a later-learned thing from Sinclair's theories? For in that moment of mind-tremor it was a torrent of men from her own land—pale and pinched and padded—who bore down upon her. . . . Then that passed. She stood shaking, but seeing clearly again.

Two score or more of them, tall and golden-brown, not one of them under six feet in height. Some of them mere boys; no old men. And their faces! They were the faces of no savages of whom she had ever heard or read: broad, comely, high-cheek-boned, some with black eyes and some with blue, and one she noted with eyes that were vividly gray in his golden face. . . . Sinclair barking out, "Damn you!—Keep off!"

They took no notice whatever. Sir John Mullaghan put his arm round Clair, Sinclair fell back to her other side. The hunters at that maneuver halted, queried one another with surprised looks, and then burst into a loud peal of laughter.

Sinclair swung up his ax. "Keep off!"

For answer one of the hunters, armed with a piece of wood shaped like a boomerang, laughed in the American's face and came casually forward under the threat of the ax—so close did he come that he stood not three feet away. Clair stared up at him, saw him young, with white teeth uncovered in an enjoying grin.

Sir John's arm shot past her, gripping Sinclair's just as it was about to descend.

"Keep steady, Doctor Sinclair. We can't do anything. . . Ah, it's too late."

For the young hunter had wheeled round at a call from his companions. Most of them had halted in attitudes of casual surprise, of cheerful indifference, but three of them, older men, were poising their spears, warningly. They called something again, and the young man, the mirth falling from his face, drew back. Unexpectedly Sinclair dropped his ax and stood staring stupidly.

Next moment, apparently galvanized into action by nothing more than a cooperative impulse, the hunters swept in and surrounded them.

"They're friendly," said Sir John. "Keep cool, Miss Stranlay."

A hand tugged gently at the eider-down quilt draped round her shoulders. She wheeled round clutching the thing. An impudent golden face smiled down at her. Behind her came another tug, and she turned on that. The quilt was in the hands of the young hunter who had smiled under the threat of the Neanderthal ax. He dropped it, and stretched out his hands again, his eyes lighted with amused curiosity. Clair's heart contracted.

"No—no!"

The laughter of the savages echoed up the evening of the hills. The three survivors of the *Magellan's Cloud* found themselves patted and pinched and questioned in pantomine. The young hunter, smiling, put his arms around Clair, and in a sudden panic she sank her teeth into a warm, muscular, golden arm.

The savage drew back with a cry of pain. Sinclair struggled free from the group surrounding him. He glared round and caught sight of Clair.

"Miss Stranlay? What is it?"

"Nothing." She was already repentant. "I was a fool."

She bent to reclaim the eider-down. One of the hunters, like a mischievous boy, kicked it beyond her reach. Thereat Sinclair flung him nearly as far. The laughter died down. The levitated hunter picked himself up, his face black with anger. He dropped his spear, came running into the circle again, pushed his face close to Sinclair's and shouted.

"Don't touch him again, Sinclair!" Clair discovered Sir John Mullaghan, panting, standing by her side. The hunters had fallen silent, with eager, expectant faces. Sir John said, "God bless me!"

Sinclair, his head thrust forward as had been the angry hunter's, seemed to be replying to the savage in his own language—a torrent of consonants. At that the angry one suddenly smacked the American in the face and then leaped back lightly out of range. Doing so, the anger vanished from his face. He laughed. Thereupon all the others shouted with laughter as well.

The *Magellan's* survivors stared astounded.

"Must be a colony of escaped lunatics," said Sir John. "I'll try to get you that quilt, Miss Stranlay. . . . What now?"

"Utso! Utso!"

The hunters, yelling, turned and ran, all but three of them. One of these seized Sinclair's wrist, another Sir John's gesticulating the while toward the hill where the pony-battle had taken place. Clair found her right hand in the grasp of a savage whose face was vaguely familiar.

It was he of the vivid gray eyes.

He waved toward the hill, urgently. Clair, with a last desperate glance backward, pointing to the quilt. He shook his head. Next moment, in the trail of Sir John and his captor, Clair Stranlay found herself running through the evening shadows of the unknown land by the side of a golden body and dark head which stirred a misty clamor of memories.

THERE were half a dozen ponies on the hill-brow. They were no larger than Shetlands. One of them was not quite dead. As Clair and the gray-eyed hunter arrived a savage bent over the beast and poising a flint ax in his hand, neatly split its skull. Half the hunters faced outward, their flint-tipped spears held ready. Strange, gray-black things with high shoulders and dragging hind-quarters came out of the gleaming dimness, glared at the groupings of dead ponies and quick men, snarled disappointedly, and wabbled backward. A hunter made a feint with his spear at one of these unaccountable beasts.

Thereat, scrambling away like a calf, it guffawed hideously. Clair felt she was going mad, standing in the gloaming chill among these laughing savages and laughing beasts. She found Sinclair beside her, and clung to him for a moment.

"Who are they? What are they going to do?"

"Wish I knew—the giggling swine! Especially that clown who slapped my face—"

"Oh, never mind your face."

"I'm sorry." Stiffly.

They looked at each other. Clair began to giggle. The American still scowled with twitching face. She realized he was almost as hysteri-

cal as she was. Realization was somehow sobering. A hunter bending
over the carcass of a pony, pushed his bearded face toward them, grinning inquisitively as though desirous of sharing a joke. Sir John Mullaghan struggled to their side, though no one made any effort to detain him.

"Sinclair, since you know their language—"

"Oh, yes, and what language is it?" Clair also had remembered.

"I don't know. I've no memory of hearing it before. But when that
circus clown came jabbering I found myself—answering him."

"But you must know what you answered."

"I don't. . . . Good God, are we to stand here while I'm put through
an examination in linguistics? Stop that damned giggling, Miss Stranlay.
. . . I'll ask them where they're going to take us—"

"No need," said the armaments manufacturer.

Nor was there. The hunters, half of them laden with portions of
pony-carcass, began to move down the southward brow of the hill. They
seemed to have no leader. The move was made in a drift of mutual
convenience. A large elderly man, over-burdened, stopped beside
Sinclair and motioned unmistakably. He wanted assistance.

"I'm damned if I do," said the American.

The man showed his teeth in a grin, lingered, moved on. It was almost
dark. A hunter with his spear slung on his arm by a thong caught Sir
John and Sinclair by the arms and urged them down the hillside.

Looking after them, it struck Clair, absurdly, that he was doing the
thing in sheer friendliness. . . . Next moment she found herself alone
on the hill-brow with the beasts, now a dark mass like a moving carpet,
snuffling up the hill toward her. She would have run but that a hand
came over her shoulder, and she almost screamed at that. It was the
gray-eyed hunter. He was evidently the rearguard!

The savage left her. Fearfully, she heard the sound of a furious
scuffle, the impact of blows. The hunter returned, breathing heavily,
glancing over his shoulder. He caught her arm anxiously. They began
to run down-hill together. Thereat a wurr of protest behind them changed into a scamper of many paws and a blood-freezing bay of laughter.

Sinclair, Sir John and the others had disappeared. Clair ran blindly
in the darkness over grass and things that were probably bush-roots, for
she stumbled on them. Behind, the pattering sound gained volume. Clair
understood. The man beside her could run as fast as the beasts by whom
they were being pursued. She was delaying him. She shook her arm free.

"Go on, you idiot, then! I can't."

For answer, still holding her hand, he swung to the right. Clair
heard the scratch and scrape of the wheeling pack behind them. The

hunter's hand shot up and gripped her wrist.

Next moment they trod vacancy.

Clair heard a feeble little ghost of a scream come from her own lips. She curved her body automatically and next moment struck water—water she could not see. Down and down, with burning eyeballs. Something tearing at her, something holding her. . . She found herself on the surface—the surface of a river it must be, for the current was strong—trying to swim and hampered in the effort by the grip of the hunter.

She tried to wrench her arm free, and then immediately stopped, realizing that he evidently knew in which direction to swim. A short distance away a snuffling clamor and bestial laughter grew fainter. Clair's knee struck soggy yielding ground. They crawled throught swamp; scrambled up an incline. Clair fell on the ground, panting. It was black as pitch. The savage was the vaguest shadow. He pulled at her shoulder impatiently, saying incomprehensible things. She raised her head.

Quite near at hand was the glow of five great fires.

SO IT seemed to Clair then, looking at the bright segmenting of the eastern night. But she was mistaken. There were five great openings into the cave, and the segmented glow had birth and being in a multitude of fires. The light grew brighter as she and the gray-eyed hunter climbed from the river.

Far in ages past that river had driven through a higher channel in the limestone bowels of the hillside; once it must have flowed eastward, an underground river. Then, in some catastrophic spate, it had burst those stygian bonds, broken free in an acre-wide vomit of great limestone boulders, and then sunk and sunk, sweeping eastward and downward till it flowed, in rough parallel, a good hundred yards from the gaping cavern mouths that marked the river bank of the original channel.

The catastrophe had left a great cave, at some points narrow, at others wide and sweeping into a glow-softened darkness; fires burned in remote sub-caves far into the rock. . . . Clair stood in the wash of light, looking at a scene as remote from the life and times of her country as it was remote from all pictures she had ever built in imagination of the life of the savage.

There were perhaps two hundred or less human beings in that immense abandoned channel of the underground river. More than half were women and children. Some were grouped round the innumerable small fires, some lay flat and apparently asleep on skins by those fires, some stood in groups—surely in gossip!

Ten yards from Clair an old man squatted, his graying hair falling over his eyes, and, in the unchancy light of the fires, smote with a mallet at a nodule of bright flint. The staccato blows rose at regular intervals, high about the hum of the cavern.

A voice called something from the group round the nearest fire, and Clair's hunter touched her arm and she found herself walking across the hard uneven floor of the cave into the concentrated astounded stare of four hundred eyes. Then (so it seemed to her) the whole cave rose en masse and precipitated itself up on her.

She said, frightenedly, so frightened that she merely said it, not screamed it, "Sinclair."

A man touched her hair, found it unbelievable, ruffled it wildly, laughed. Two women stroked her arm. Someone pinched her. A boy who might have been five years old slipped through the forest of legs and clasped Clair's knees, so that she almost fell. She clenched her fists and struck one of the women in the mouth.

At that the touching hands left her. The babble hushed. The laughing curious eyes darkened. And from somewhere Sir John's voice called:

"Don't do that, Miss Stranlay! They don't mean any harm."

So Clair had realized. It was impossible, but it was a fact. The golden-skinned people were as friendly as they were unreticent. Clair did something then that was an inspiration—leaned forward to the woman she had hit and kissed her on her bruised mouth.

"I—I'm sorry."

Thus haltingly (and appropriately, she was afterward to think) her greeting to that world from her own. For answer the brown-haired woman put up her arms, and kissed her in return.

Clair found her hand seized by the woman. She found herself being led away toward a fire burning solitary in a subcave of the great rock chamber. She found herself sitting on a badly-cured skin, with beside her the woman whom she had hit and kissed bending over the fire, toasting a long gray fish in much the same fashion as Sinclair had toasted the horse-meat.

The American and Sir John were hasting toward her, threading the dottings of fires. Behind them followed the gray-eyed savage.

"Where did you get to, Miss Stranlay?"

Sinclair was unreasonably angry. Also, it seemed to her he was still hysterical. He kept glancing from the right to left, toward the cave-mouths, the cavern-ceiling, the groups of the golden-skinned. He waited for no answer, but gripping his head with his hands, half-turned away. Clair thought, disturbedly, "Good gracious, what's the fuss—now we've fallen among these nice natives? They'll guide us to a town or a trading-post in a day or so." She smiled up at the two of them.

"Having a walk with a gentleman friend. There he is behind you."

The hunter came up, unsmiling. He looked from Clair to Sinclair, from Sinclair to Sir John. Then his gray eyes came back to Clair questioningly. He made a motion from her to Sinclair.

She said to Sinclair: "What?"

The American stared at her and the hunter abstractedly. He was certainly on the verge of a breakdown. He said, "Eh?" and then, to the savage, a bark of intelligibility. The savage answered.

"He wants to know if you are my wife."

Clair sat up with some abruptness. "What have you told him?"

Sir John Mullaghan said very evenly: "I think Sinclair had better say yes, Miss Stranlay."

Clair found the three of them watching her—Sinclair with a strange dazed look on his face. ("Not thinking of me at all.") The woman toasting the fish looked up with wondering, friendly eyes. Clair thought, "Silly ass—go on, agree!" and so thinking found herself for some reason shaking her head at the gray-eyed hunter.

He smiled gravely, nodded and walked away. Clair, with a little catch of breath, watched him go.

T HAT question was to return with frightening intensity a few hours later.

The fires had died down considerably. Heaped with damp grass and heavy boughs they smoldered with the smell of garden rubbish burned in an English garden. The smoke drifted out of the circle-radiance of each fire, coiled to the room, and then, in an army of ragged banners, went north into the unexplored darkness of the ancient river-bed. Outside, a wind had risen that soughed eerily among the stars. On either side of the fires the hunters and their women slept.

Sir John Mullaghan had emerged once from the bizarre cavern background and the distant fire where he had been adopted.

"Comfortable, Miss Stranlay? If you want Sinclair or myself during the night, just shout. One of us will keep awake."

"Oh, don't. I'm sure we're safe enough. Who on earth *are* these people, Sir John?"

"I've no idea—unless I'm to accept Sinclair's new theory. Perfectly mad." He stared down at her with something like horror on his gentle face. "At least, I hope to God it's mad. . . . We'll discuss the matter tomorrow. Have you noticed the paintings on the roof?"

"Paintings?"

"Look. Amazing things, aren't they?" He muttered to himself distractedly. "And the final proof for Sinclair's sanity. . . . Oh, they can't be," He shook himself. "Good night, Miss Stranlay."

"Good night, Sir John."

She had stared after him, troubled and puzzled. Sinclair? . . . And then her eyes had turned to the wild beauty and vigor of the painted beasts that stood and charged and fled in panic flight amid the coiling of the fire-smoke. Here was their saber-tooth, in black and gray, yonder, a red mammoth; center of the great arch of the cave chamber a nightmare monster bunched in polychrome, gigantically, for an attack. . . . Savages—and these paintings! Where were they? What country was this?

She turned now, the heavy pelt of an unknown animal beneath her, and lay on her right shoulder. She pulled another skin, long-haired and warm, up to her neck, and lay sleepless, looking down the stretch of the caves. Savages. Awful people. Only—neither savage nor awful.

A yard away the woman she had hit stood by the side of a broad-chested hunter with one eye and a face disfigured as though half of it had been torn away. He had come into the cave while the woman had been feeding Clair on a piece of fish and a handful of green, rushlike things. He was evidently a late arrival from the hunt, and the woman his wife.

Clair had shuddered at sight of his face, and then saw that the hideous grimace on it was an interested smile.

A second later Clair looked over her shoulder at the hunter and his squaw in the cave silence. They might have been Iseult and Tristan together in that unshielded embrace.

She closed her eyes—and instantly opened them again. Somewhere close to the cave-mouths a savage snarling had broken out. Clair raised herself on her elbow. She could just see through the nearest entrance, In the pearl starshine stalked two dim shapes, long-bodied, sinster. Were they coming into the cave?

They growled again, and she realized the brutes were hesitating, seeking to summon up courage for just such a raid. But while she thought so a figure beside one of the far fires arose, stirred the fire near to him to a blaze, and with blazing torch came sleepily down the length of the main cave, stirring each fire. Lights yellow and red and lilac fountained with much crackle and twinkle. The beasts in the starlight vanished. Clair sank down again, watching the man with the torch.

He stopped beside her fire, stirring it as he had done the others, but more cautiously. Then he laid down the torch and crossed to where Clair lay. She closed her eyes, fast.

With that blinding of herself the silence of the night and cave fell upon her senses acutely, like a sharp pain. It was an actual, physical relationship, not of hearing alone, this silence. The crackling fires had ceased their crackling, burning now in a steady loom. Outside, the wind had died away, perhaps awaiting the moonrise—or even the dawn, for how could one know the hour? And bending over her was a savage.

She bit her lips, hearing the fervid beating of her own heart. He also would hear it, and at that thought she tried, foolishly, to ease its noise.

Should she shout for Sinclair?

She opened her eyes. She knew him then. It was the gray-eyed hunter. And it was some one else: the face of the boy who had died outside Mametz bent over her in dim scrutiny.

So, for a moment, then he turned and went, and Clair laid her head in her arms and slipped into unconsciousness.

CHAPTER SEVEN—A *Slip in the Time-Spirals*

IT WAS next afternoon.

Clair Stranlay lay sleeping in the sunlight of the bluff that fronted the caves across the river. She was high up there, and had found a place where the sear grass was less coarse than usual, and soft to lie on. She had not intended to sleep, but to lie taking mental stock of the forenoon's impressions, to watching the unending play of life in the cave-mouths opposite.

So, indeed, she had done for a little after climbing the bluff, seeing the remote golden figures of hunters or women stroll out against the limestone pillars of their habitations, seeing the moving, hasting, recumbent dots that were children sprayed out in all directions from the cave-mouths to the river.

Then sleep had come upon her, unawares, yet gently, so that even sleeping she was conscious that she slept and slept comfortably.

So the newcomers over the grass, from the opposite way up the bluff that she had taken, did not greatly startle her. She opened clear undrowsy eyes and watched Sir John Mullaghan and the American sit down beside her, one on either side.

"You've been a long time," she said. "If there is time in this place."

The two men glanced at each other, swiftly, queerly, then looked away again. They said nothing. Sir John passed his hand over his gray hair in characteristic gesture. He had begun to fray badly, Sir John.

He still had his trousers and coat, but the trousers were now shorts, the coat lacked sleeves. Sinclair—

Clair glanced at herself, and made hasty redrapings of her rags. "Goodness, our tailors will do a thriving trade when we do get back!"

"If we ever get back," said Sinclair.

Clair had half-expected some such remark. Yet it startled her. "So there's something behind their friendliness? Do they—do they intend to do something to us?"

"Eh?" The American looked blank for a moment. Grinned without mirth. "Oh, the cooking-pot or something like that? I imagine they've never dreamed of cannibalism. No, it's not that. We're prisoners—but only as a result of the most fantastic accident. Frankly, Miss Stranlay, I don't think there's any chance of us getting back to civilization again."

"But—we're not going to stay here always? We can start out exploring again, and we're bound to reach some place in touch with civilization. Some time."

"I doubt it."

"Why?"

"Because I don't think there's such a thing as civilization in existence."

Clair nodded, chewing a stalk of grass. "I know. I felt like that last night. . . . But it's only an illusion we play with, of course."

Sir John struck in quietly. "Sinclair means it seriously, Miss Stranlay."

CLAIR sat up, looking at them both.

"Seriously? But—We came out of—civilization five or six days ago."

Sinclair drew up his knees in front of him and clasped them. "I don't mean anything illusory, symbolic or allegorical when I say there's no such thing as civilization. I just mean it, Miss Stranlay. There's no such thing; there won't be any such thing for thousands of years."

"Perhaps you'd better detail all the evidence, Sinclair."

"Yes." The American turned his square, firmly modeled head. Clair, troubled though she was, had a little shock of enlightenment. Of course—that was it! The hunters had heads like that; "Let's go back to the beginning of all these happenings, Miss Stranlay—"

"Oh, let's. But why?"

"A minute. Remember what happened on board the *Magellan's Cloud*? First, there was that submarine earthquake. Then the airship's wireless failed to get any message from outside, though the set was quite undamaged. Then it grew inexplicably cold for that time of the year, and we saw islands appearing in mid-Atlantic—and quite evidently islands not newly risen from the sea. And then—the moon appearing at the full, though no moon was due for another five days."

Clair wriggled herself flat again in the sunlight. She felt a strange uneasiness. "Yes, I remember all that. And it was a different moon."

"It still is a different moon," said Sir John. "I went out of the cave early this morning and saw it. Intense volcanic activity must still be going on up there."

"More than likely. You've got all these facts, Miss Stranlay? Then, the *Magellan's Cloud* was wrecked against a mountain in a land that couldn't exist. . . . We spent a deal of argument in the last few days trying to guess what the land was. I suppose it was necessary to argue to keep sane. I was never very convinced by my own arguments. Now we've had time to think, it's plain that the airship didn't diverge sufficiently from its course—or go at such an altered speed—as to reach back either to Africa or forward to Canada or Patagonia."

"Yes. But we're somewhere."

"Obviously. But it isn't any place you ever heard of, is it? It is, in the geography of the twentieth century, an impossible place, because the airship couldn't have reached it."

Clair had begun to see. "Then—it's a new country, somewhere in the middle of the Atlantic? . . . But that's nonsense. It's too big not to have been discovered before. It must be as big as ancient Atlantis."

There was silence. Sir John had turned his face to the blow of the sunlight wind. Sinclair spoke.

"Exactly. That is where I'm convinced we are—in that continent which once filled the eastern trough of the Atlantic."

CLAIR covered her ears. "Once filled it? Stop, please. . . . I feel as muzzy as a fly in honey. Once. . . . That was thousands of years ago. Atlantis. How can we be in Atlantis now?"

"Because the now is thousands of years ago."

Clair laughed and patted her ears. "There's something wrong with my hearing. You'll have to examine my ears."

"It sounds very confusing, Miss Stranlay, but I think Doctor Sinclair's cumulative evidence is unimpeachable."

"Evidence of what?"

"Let me go on with the evidence first," Sinclair said quietly. "We three survived the *Magellan's* wreck, we found a plateau practically without human beings in its northernmost part. And there was a long mountain chain that must be a vent of the central fires of the earth, with thirteen unknown volcanoes on it."

"Were there thirteen? I never counted."

"Yes. Toward the end of the plateau we sheltered in a cave and were almost killed by a saber-toothed tiger. And in the cave I found the bones and skull—fresh bones and fresh skull, not fossils—of a Neanderthal man. We came down from the plateau and were chased by a mammoth. We saw an Irish elk, and, late last night, hyaenodons. All these animals —and the Neanderthal man—had long been extinct before the twentieth century. And, last of all, we are made prisoners by these people"—he waved his hand toward the caves—"whom at first I thought were merely an unknown tribe of savages."

"And aren't they?'

"I don't think so. I know what their language is and, and, why I answer in it so readily. It's Basque—an elementary and elemental form of Basque. My mother was Basque. I haven't spoken the language since childhood, but last evening found myself speaking and thinking in it half unconsciously. . . . It's the loneliest language in twentieth-century Europe, as I suppose you know. No affinities to any other, just as the Basques have no apparent racial affinity to any existing group. It's been speculated that they're the pure descendants of the Cro-Magnards— you've heard of them?"

It sounded to Clair foolishly remote from their trouble of finding a way back to a knowable coast and civilization. She wrinkled her sunburned brows. "I think so. Yes—I went picnicking to the Cro-Magnon caves once and drank bad Moselle there. They were the Stone Age people who painted all those French and Spanish caves, weren't they?" Painters! Apparent enlightment came on her. "And you think our hunters are a stray tribe of Basques?"

"No, I don't. I think they're proto-Cro-Magnards—ancestors of the French Cro-Magnards and remote ancestors to the twentieth-century Basques."

"Ancestors?"

Sir John patted her shoulder. "I think you'd have done better to tell her your theory right out, Sinclair—rather than lead up to it."

Still, miraculously, Sinclair kept his temper. "All right. Plainly, then, Miss Stranlay, and fantastic as it may sound, I believe we're not in the twentieth century at all—that through some inexplicable accident connected with that submarine earthquake the *Magellan's Cloud* fell out of the twentieth century."

"What is it, then?" Clair heard her voice in the strangest whisper.

"I don't know. But from all the evidences I should think we're somewhere in the autumn of a year between thirty and twenty thousand years before the birth of Christ."

"IT WILL always remain unreal—and oh, nonsensically impossible to believe!"

More than two hours had gone by. Clair's face was more pallid than either of the men had ever seen it, and indeed it had required something of her disbelief and horror to make them realize the thing themselves.

"Are these people unreal?"·

Clair looked down. "No, they are real enough." She spoke in a low voice, so that they scarcely caught her words. "It's—a devil of a thing. I don't believe I'll think about it much . . . if I can. Or at least not deliberately try to go mad. . . . All this stuff about the time-spirals and retrocognitive memory—maths have always given me a headache. The world used always, I thought, to roll along a straight line called Time, instead of looping the loop with a thousand ghosts of itself before and after it. And none of them the ghost, and none the reality."

Sir John said: "I'm not a mathematician either, Miss Stranlay. But I take it they're all realities in the loop-spirals. And for a second—at that moment of the submarine earthquake—two of the loops touched, and the *Magellan's Cloud* was scraped off one on to the other?"

"Like a fly off a pat of butter?"

"Something like that." He smiled at her from behind his grizzled beard.

That was better. The Cockney was coming to her help. Clair said:

"Please. It's a September afternoon in London now. There are dead leaves in the parks, and people at the Zoo drinking tea under the leaves. And motor-buses going round Trafalgar Square and pigeons twittering on the roofs of St. Martin's in the Field. And there's been an accident in Hammersmith Broadway, and the policeman is shooting back the crowd. And Big Ben says it's twenty past three, and there's an unemployment procession, and there's Bond Street and shops and queues in Leicester Square for an Edgar Wallace play. . . .

"And it's not now. It won't happen for twenty-five thousand years. Year after year. I've been speaking just a minute. And it's a long time until sunset. And till the sunset of tomorrow. And until the winter comes here on these caves. And until the spring of next year. Year after year, till we're all three dead. And years after that, till this country's dead and no one really believes it existed. And years after that, with spring and summer and birds over the hills and belling deer, and people in love, and the babies becoming old men and women, and dying, and their descendants seeing another spring.

"An Ice Age coming—slowly, through thousands of years. And passing away through thousands more. And at the end of that time—London

will still be in the future. . . .. It's not now, it never can be for us, nor
for any one now alive. . . ."

Her voice had risen; it cracked on the last word. Sinclair was on his
feet. He took her by the shoulder and shook her. Laughing and crying,
she stared up in his eyes. Sir John half stood up also, made to interfere,
refrained. Clair struggled. Her hysteria died away. Sinclair's fingers
relaxed. Clair found herself staring at him resentfully, flushed.

"You beast!"

He was panting. "Anything you like. I tried to be an effective counter-
irritant. Feel better?"

Clair shuddered. "Don't look at me, you two, for a bit."

They didn't. After a little they heard her say, "Sorry I went like that,
especially after my promise."

"I felt like going that way myself last night."

"Did you?"

The American nodded. "And we're to make a compact, all three. If
one of us ever feels that way again, we're to get to the other two at once.
Promise?"

Sinclair nodded to Clair's spoken reply and Sir John's nod, and they
said nothing for a little. Clair's mind felt as though it were slowly re-
covering from a surgical operation. *Atlantis!* She said, "And what are we
going to do?"

"What is there we can do?"

This was Sinclair. Clair turned her eyes to the armaments manufacturer. He smiled at her. He looked ill, she reflected. He said gently:

"At least, we have all our lives to live—now, as in that time that is
not yet, that time that is thousands of years away. And they are our
lives."

"Oh!" Clair sat up again. "I knew there was something you two had
left unexplained. Most important of all. You can't explain it." She turned
to the American accusingly. "If these are the ancestors of the Cro-
Magnards who are to become the ancestors of the Basque—"

"And perhaps our own ancestors. Your own remote ancestor may be
one of these children playing by the river there, Miss Stranlay."

"Oh, my good God!" She was checked for a moment, and again the
curtain of horror waved before her eyes. And, queerly, something came
to her aid. It was memory of the gray-eyed hunter. "But that doesn't
matter. Won't bear thinking about. If these people are as far back in
time as you imagine—they're remoter from civilization than any savage
of the twentieth century."

"Far remoter," said Sinclair. "Their weapons and implements are paleolithic flints. They seem to have no knowledge of even the elements of an agriculture. They haven't even arrived at the idea of storing water in calabashes—as I found to my discomfort last night."

"They've no tribal organization," said Sir John. "That is plain enough already. None of the ultimate divisions of power and responsibility have yet been evolved."

"But—*your* theories, Sir John, and yours, Doctor Sinclair. . . . Where is the raving Old Man with his harem of wives? And where's all the cruelty and fear and horror? They're not 'savages; they're clean and kindly children. Listen!"

Some jest of the caves. The shout of laughter came up to them on the bluff-head. Both the men were silent. Clair said: "So it must be the twentieth century and Patagonia or some such place after all."

THE American shook his head. "It's not the twentieth century: our data is stable enough. It's just that all the history books and all the anthropological theories of the twentieth century tell the most foolish lies ever invented. It's just that Sir John Mullaghan and I and thousands more have been victims of the shoddiest scientific lie ever imposed on human credulity. . . . These proto-Cro-Magnards, these earliest true men on earth—absolutely without culture and apparently absolutely without superstitious fears, cruelties, or class-divisions. It means that Rousseau was right (or will be right? How is one to think of it?) and the twentieth-century evolutionists all wrong."

Clair said steadily: "These—like our ancestors; perhaps some of them our own ancestors. . . ." For a moment it seemed to her that her two companions were ghouls squatting beside her in the sunlight. "And I knew it—women always knew it! But you two and the thousands of others who lead the world swore that men were natural murderers: you killed five million in France to prove your theories. All through history you've been doing it. . . . The boy who died on the wire outside Mametz —he was one of those hunters, I saw his own face last night. And you told him he was a murderous beast by nature and ancestry!"

She was aware of the armaments manufacturer looking at her, doubt and gray horror in his face. "Perhaps this is only a stray tribe of primitives unlike all others."

"No." Sinclair spoke. Abruptly, as with an effort. "They are no stray tribe. You are right, Miss Stranlay. You are woman, for that matter, or fifty tortured centuries accusing us. . . . And we've no defense. We never tried to find out the real facts of human nature. . . . By God, but some did! I've just remembered. There was a new school of thought.

The Diffusionist. And we thought them fantastic dreamers!"

"What did they dream?"

"Why, that primitive man was no monster, that it was the early civilizations and their offshoots that bedeviled him. If a Diffusionist were here at the moment he would say that these are men as nature intended them to be. So they will continue for thousands of years till, by an accident in the Nile Valley, agriculture and its attendant religious rites will be evolved. And from that accident in 4000 B.C. will rise, transforming the world, the castes and gods, the warrior and slave, the cruelties and cannibalisms, Sir John Mullaghan's armaments, the war that murdered your fiancé, and my League of Militant Pacifists."

They stared at Clair uncomfortably in the bright sunshine. A party of hunters came over the eastward hills—golden figures against a golden background. They were singing, these dawn-men—godless and fearless and hateless and glorious, Sinclair thought, they who should have slouched through the sunlight obsessed and hideous animals! . . . Sir John was grayly conscious of Clair's silent figure.

"But I still don't understand. If this is the world of twenty-five thousand B.C., as we've calculated, what is its population? Are there other men? Is there a Europe? And that Neanderthal skull—it didn't belong to a species of man like one of these hunters, surely?"

The American made an abrupt, half-despairing gesture.

"How can we know—now—since all our other beliefs about these times go *phut*? Something like this, I imagine: Atlantis here is a great waste of land, the youngest and most unstable of the continents. It must stretch out at points almost across to the Antilles and America. And wandering through it are possibly a few scarce family groups like our hunters. Possibly—but our hunters may be the only true men as yet in existence.

"They must have been wandering this land for thousands of years. In the east there, toward Europe and in Europe itself, there are Neanderthal men—unhuman, a primitive experiment by Nature in the making of man. They also must be few enough in number, though their species probably spreads far into Asia and Africa.

"And somewhere in Central and Southeastern Asia at this moment may be other family groups of true men, not so very different from these golden cavemen of ours, slowly wandering westward. . . . There is an Ice Age coming, a few thousand years hence, and at the end of it the Neanderthalers will die out and these hunters, or rather their descendants, reach Europe and spread over it, intermarry with those remote kinsmen of theirs from Asia. . . . Something like that."

He jumped to his feet. "Oh, by God, if one could only tell them—

those hunters of ours!"

"Tell them what?" asked Sir John.

"History—the world that is to be. Remember that kindly chap that took you and me prisoners—we thought we were prisoners and we weren't at all. He's never heard the words for war or prison. Or that hunter who brought Miss Stranlay to the caves. . . . If they knew what their children there in the sunlight inherit—thousands of years away!

"All the bloody butcheries of the battlefields, the tortures and mutilatings of the cities still unbuilt, the blood-sacrifices of the Aztec altars, those maimed devils who die in the coal mines of Europe. . . ." He looked down at Clair. "You were born in the slums—thirty thousand years in the future. Think that it still has to happen—for these."

Clair said, in a pale, quiet voice: "Will you two leave me alone? Oh, I won't go mad again."

"Don't stay too late. We'll watch for you from the cave."

"All right, Sir John."

She heard the *scuff-scuff* of their receding footsteps. She was alone.

"WHAT am I to do?" she thought. "Oh, my good God, what am I to do? If we're here forever—but I can't! I may live to be a hundred—days and days and months and years—among horse-flesh and fires. No books. Never have the fun of correcting my own proofs. Or lying on a soft clean bed. Or smoking cigarettes. Never talk to the people who like my kind of jokes, or be clever and bright. Or wear pretty clothes and have men admire me. And be safe—safe and secure. . . ."

The grass rustled under her as she lay and wept, terrified. She closed her eyes, tightly, to make sure that this country and the American's talk were all part of a dream. Ever so tightly. In a moment, when she opened them, she'd know. It couldn't be, it couldn't be. . . . She opened her eyes on the afternoon of the pale Atlantean hills.

"Let's think calmly, then. If this were only a novel—one of the kind you've wanted to write for a holiday. Think that this isn't yourself; only your heroine. It's she who's lying on a hill above a lost Atlantis cave, watching the children of the dawnmen playing by a lost river. . . . And you're comfortable in your Kensington study, planning out the synopsis. What's she going to do next? How's she going to live? She *must* live—you'd never be mean enough to kill her off. But *how?*"

It was late in the afternoon now—those afternoons that seemed to contract so steadily with the wearing of the week. She saw the smoke far up the opposite hillside—from some high vent that aerated the caves —thicken from pale blue to violet black. They were building up the fires.

Soon the main body of the hunters, that had left at dawn, would return.
The individual hunters must long ago have returned. Sinclair and Sir
John waiting for her. Hungry. Hungry herself.

She stood up. The wind had turned cooler. She shivered. Her ragged
jacket flapped, and the pajama-trouser blew against her legs.

CHAPTER EIGHT—For the Dark Days

THAT night the rain set in, blowing gustily into the mouths of the
caves, so that the flames of the fires danced and spat and flickered,
and long serpent-shapes of smoke wound and whorled everywhere.
Amid them blew sharp piercing shafts of wind, and Clair began to realize
something of the life of those people in the winter months.

She lay wakeful beside her fire, and Sinclair, who could not sleep
either, came over to her while the beating gusts shook the limestone
hills and moaned far in the subterranean depths of the river-bed.

"Shocking night."

Clair stirred the fire gently with a bough, and nodded to him. He
stood looking into the fire himself.

Clair wound the odorous bearskin more closely round herself.

"Let me feel your pulse," he said.

He did. It seemed quite normal. She startled him with a question.
"Do you think we'll pull through the winter months—especially Sir John?"

"What?"

"Oh, you know. *You* will, I think. You have physique for it, and most
of the other advantages. I may—through the accident that winter-bathing
was my hobby—though goodness knows I feel like a white snail among
all these golden people."

"You looked lovely enough."

He said this impersonally. Clair nodded. "I know I'm not unsightly.
But, best-selling never trained me for a winter in Atlantis."

He was silent. He bent down to place a burning twig more evenly.
The wind whoomed, blowing his hair and beard, as Clair saw looking
up at him from the shelter of her bearskin. In shadow and in flickering
light the Cro-Magnards slept disregarding rain and squall—all, except
three very young babies who wailed softly in the far corner of the cave.

These apart, even the very youngest slept soundly. Outside, against
the cave-mouths, the wavering curtains of rain. . . . Atlantis! Lost in
Atlantis and pre-history! Clair, forgetting the silent Sinclair, leaned on
an elbow, gazing round at the sleeping hunters with golden easy bodies.

Those cavemen, the men of the dawn! And suddenly it was to her as though they lay dead, they and their women and children, and over them indeed came stalking those ghoulish shapes with which the world remote in the future was to identify them—great beasts, slime-dripping, with fetid jaws and rheumy eyes, tearing at the throats of these dead men of the dawn, mangling and destroying and befouling the human likeness from the lovely limbs and faces. . . .

"You're sleepy now. Good night."

"Oh—I was dreaming awake. Good night—it's ridiculous to say Doctor Sinclair. What is your name?"

"Keith."

"Good night, Keith."

"Good night, Clair."

"Awful. How it's raining! Drumming like a London roof under rain, almost. London roofs—but you mustn't think of them. Nor all your London days. Over, all days, very soon, I suppose."

She grew wakeful again at that thought. Sinclair had gone without answering her question. Over: all the bright burnished hours, the days of summers and autumns, the good things to eat, the ease and pleasantness. . . . To come to an end and a blinding in darkness at last, somewhere, in some dark cave, without medical attention or understanding. And some one, unless Sinclair or Sir John was still alive, would carry her body outside the range of the caves; and leave it for a beast to devour.

She looked, and so for long until the fire died continued to look, into a night that was a pit of terror.

B UT that next dawn—
    She awoke luxuriously, in the embrace of a strange, secret exaltation. Why? Something awaiting her? She put aside the fur and got up and shivered in the dawn chill, and saw then that it was barely dawn.

No one stirred. Far at the farthest fire the watcher of the fires was smoothing a stick with a flint. He heard her, lightly though she walked, and looked round, and flung back his hair from his face, and smiled. A boy. She smiled and warmed herself by the fire of another household.

Then she went to the nearest mouth of the cavern, and at her appearance the sun that had been hesitating behind the hills came over them, and she stood and shivered with pleasure in its first beams. The guard hunter came to her side; said something unintelligible; motioned toward the river. A lion and a lioness, gray beasts rather than tawny in that light, were standing watching them, not twenty yards away.

The hunter gestured with the half-smoothed bough in his hand. Promptly the lion disappeared through the soft wet grass. The lioness growled and stalked after him despondently.

The caves began to stir. The women awoke and fed their babies. The men arose and drifted about and were scolded, and grinned, and crowded the cave-mouths as though in casual gossip. Clair saw Sir John Mullaghan rising, with some appearance of chilled joints, from a heap of boughs. A Cro-Magnard helped him up.

A frizzling smell began to pervade the cavern. Breakfast. It was deer-flesh, cooked in the same monotonous way as always. Frying-pans, pots and pantries were as unknown as gods, chancels and torture-chambers. Afterward the Cro-Magnards would wander down to the river in twos and threes, and drink.

The men went away in the early morning, after drinking at the river and indulging in some horseplay when three of them were thrown into the water, and the others—apparently in a mood of self-retaliation—flung themselves in on top. Watching them, Clair said to Sir John, "But I thought swimming was a very artificial acquirement of human beings."

"Perhaps this family group has wandered from the shore of some inland seat in Atlantis. They're certainly very cleanly, though it's plain it's not because of any code. They are because they enjoy it."

"Where's Keith Sinclair?"

Sir John smiled. "He's going out with the hunters."

Clair saw him approaching then. It was apparently for him that the watcher of the fires had been smoothing the bough through the night. He carried that bough now, straightened, and with a carefully knapped sliver of flint wedged and bound in it. Clair reached out her hand and took the thing and examined it, and some of the women came and looked at the three of them smilingly.

The American nodded as he handed it back. There was a flush on his dour face, a sparkle in his eyes. "I suspect I'll be the worst kind of amateur. At stalking as well as running—in spite of my atavistic legs."

"Atavistic?"

"Hadn't you noted it? I'm fairly Cro-Magnard altogether in physiognomy. And the twentieth century seems to have guessed correctly from study of the fossil remains of these people found in the French caves that their long shin bones were developed by racing game on foot. . . . By the by, this is a feast day."

"Feast?" Sir John, a grotesque figure in his rags, had sat down. He smiled at them, grayly. "I'm sorry, Miss Stranlay. I'm still a trifle upset internally. . . . Did you say a feast, Sinclair?"

"Yes."

"But from what you were telling me of the Diffusionist theory of history last night I understood that ritual feasts came only with civilization?"

"There seem to be two exceptions. Perhaps they're memories of the old pre-human mating seasons. In spring and autumn they occur, as far as I can gather from the old flint-knapper, Aitz-kore; and the autumn one comes after the first night of rain."

"What's it for?" Clair asked.

"It's the time, I understand, when the men and women choose their mates for the winter—or those already mated exchange. Sir John and I will take you out for a walk when it comes off, if you like."

"No. If we're here for the remainder of our lives that would be too suburban. . . ." She suddenly gripped his arm. "There's my hunter."

No other. Clair had not seen him all the day before. He went and sat down by a fire and ate some scraps of venison surviving the breakfast. A baby came and fell over his feet. He righted it absorbedly and put it aside. The baby procured a bone and sucked it.

"Been out on a lone trek, I should think," said the American. "They often do that, the young and unmarried, according to Aitz-kore. Wander off sometimes and don't come back. Hello, they're waiting for me!"

"Good hunting!"

"Thanks." He called over his shoulder. "Don't stray far from the caves, either of you."

Scouts had already gone. Others straggled westward by the marsh, going casually, for there was no game near at hand. The American pacifist joined a golden-skinned group and companioned them out of sight, his white skin very conspicuous. Clair looked after him, stretched luxuriously and sighed deeply. Sir John looked up inquiringly.

"Nothing, Sir John, except—did you ever sleep on Box Hill on a Sunday afternoon?

"Heat and stickiness and some one playing a melodeon, and poor life-starved louts prowling among the bushes. Goodness, the stickiness and the taste in one's mouth! When we might have been like- this. . . . Box Hill!"

Sir John also had fallen into a dream. Box Hill! His company; his constituency; that journey to America. . . . Here in the sunshine of Atlantis one began to doubt them. Had they ever been? . . . He found he had been thinking aloud. He found Clair's hand on his shoulder. Her lovely face was lighted but dreamy still.

"Perhaps they were, but—*need they ever be*? Perhaps men dreamed the wrong dream. We are such stuff of dreams. . . . Perhaps it was only a nightmare astray on Sinclair's time-spirals out of which we came. . . . It feels so here this morning. As though all the world could begin again—"

Begin again? Sir John put his head in his hands. Begin again! Who indeed knew what was possible in this fantastic adventure?—if only the pain could go and he could see it and understand it more clearly. . . . Begin again? Poets had dreamed it, and they had changed the world with other dreams. . . .

I T WAS mid-afternoon.

The caves had emptied their entire population on to the plateau east of the river bank. They had trooped out in little groups, men and women separately for once. A couple of jackals, roused from a bed of reeds, had distracted somewhat the attention of the processions, the entire tribe engaging in an idiot chase of the beasts, pelting them with stones, shouting until long after the snarling brutes were out of sight.

Clair, laughing and panting, rejoined Sir John and Sinclair.

"Feels as though I were going to the world's first picnic!"

Beyond the nullahs was a flattish stretch of grass, short-cropped perhaps in the hour-passing of some enormous herd. Right of it lay the river. Over the westward hills beyond the marsh hung the sun, high up. The gray-gold land drowsed. And the Cro-Magnards' laughter went up a little wind.

The women and children grouped themselves, sitting or standing or lying, round the eastward verge of the sward. The men held over to the other side and also lay or sat. A silence fell. The three survivors of the *Magellan's Cloud* looked at one another in some doubt; finally reached a spot that seemed neutral, neither for men nor women. They lay down, resting on their elbows. The silence went on.

Suddenly a blackbird began to pipe in a thicket near at hand, breaking the tension for the three aliens at least.

The sound had stirred the Cro-Magnards also. A man rose slowly from the midst of the male embankment, and slowly walked across toward the gathering of women. The sun glided over gray-black hair.

"It's the old flint-knapper, Aitz-kore," whispered the American.

So it was. Still the silence went on as he passed over the grass. The rustle of his passage if not his footfalls could be heard. He arrived at the end of the women's line, and slowly passed up the ranks of the women, scanning each face. They looked him in the eye. One or two of the younger ones giggled. But for the most they kept the initial silence.

Sir John whispered: "His wife is there in the middle."

Aitz-kore neared her. Clair found herself holding her breath. The flint-knapper passed the woman without a change of countenance. Something seemed to contract in Clair's throat.

Aitz-kore reached the end of the line, paused, shrugged, turned back, walked slowly over the track he had already made in the grass, his face like his name, a pointed hatchet, old and sharp. He halted in front of the woman who had been his wife. She had sat with head down-bent, but she raised it now. Clair was too far off to see her face, but she knew she was weeping. The flint-knapper held out his hand. The woman took it and rose up. A yell of delight rose from hunters and women alike.

"He's selected her again from all the women of the tribe," Sinclair explained.

The two of them walked down to the southward end of the plateau, turned leftward, in the opposite direction from the caves, and were out of sight.

Again a man crossed the open space, walked the line and made selection of a woman—a young woman, and comely. But he had less luck than Aitz-kore. The woman shook her head. The hunter, after a moment's hesitation, walked back to the place from which he had come.

It was now the woman's turn. She rose. Leisurely she crossed to the seated rows of men, hesitated not an instant, but held out her hand. Instantly a young man—a mere boy—sprang to his feet and took her hand. Again the strange cheer went up from the gathering.

The woman and boy broke into an easy, long-legged trot, southward, across the sward, and then turning east and racing for the hills. Another woman rose up and crossed toward the men's side, stopping midway to fling back a cloud of russet hair from a flushed, high-cheek-boned face.

"She has a lovely figure," said Clair.

"They all have," said Sinclair.

Golden children in the dawn of time, they paired in the afternoon sunshine and in pairs melted away into the east. Clair, warm and comfortable, found herself nodding drowsily. Every now and then, however, she would start to half-wakefulness as another shout went up, another nuptial couple wheeled out of the gathering. Suddenly, in a long quietness, she started fully awake.

"Keep cool, Miss Stranlay."

Clair raised her head. An intenser silence than ever before had fallen on the gathering. Few of the Cro-Magnards were sitting now. All stood to look. And the reason was the gray-eyed hunter, Aerte.

He walked from the far end of the men's line. His head was a little down-bent, as though in deep thought. Under his left arm was his spear. Disregarding the waiting line of women he came, straight toward where the three survivors of the airship's wreck lay,

Clair thought, breathlessly: "Cooler, now. Must get back to the caves

soon. Sir John—wonder if he's feeling better? . . . Defense. Not thinking.
Taking no heed." But in some fashion she felt as though she had just
finished running an exhausting race. Sinclair, his eyes on the hunter, said:

"Just shake your head, Clair. There's no compulsion among these
people."

But Clair's head he saw was as down-bent as the hunter's own. She
saw the nearing feet in the grass, but nothing more. And then he was
close; had halted. She raised her head.

They looked at each other for a long time. She heard the American
say something; something quite incomprehensible because of that drumming noise in her ears. She was looking up, even in the still sunshine,
not in the face of Aerte alone. Her heart was wrung with a sudden wild
pain of recognition, and then that passed, leaving a tingling as of blood,
long congealed, that flowed again. . . . A gentle voice came nearer and
nearer out of the silence. Sir John's.

"He'll go away. It's just that he doesn't realize that you are different."

"I'm glad."

They saw her swing to her feet. She stood beside the hunter.

"Miss Stranlay!"

There was urgency and appeal in the simultaneous cry. Clair looked
back at them, shook her head. They had grown the mistiest of images.

And then she put her hand in the hand of the hunter, Aerte, felt that
—and close on hers, felt herself drawn forward, heard a groan from Sir
John Mullaghan as she and the hunter moved away in the direction of
the other promised mates.

RAIN came on again that night. Winter was not far off from Atlantis.
Distant in the north the volcanoes smoked, and some times, in the
lifting clouds of rain, could be glimpsed as the beating of damp beacons
remote in the mirk. Clair, lying sleepless, saw them, pregnant, dark
blossoms high up in the sky. Remote there was the plateau crossed by
herself and Sinclair and Sir John only three days ago. Fantastic journey.
Fantastic climax to it, this. . . . The hunter stirred, dreamlessly, dark
and golden, and she peered at him, then at the passing curtains of rain.

A lover—a chosen husband—for the dark days! A lover dead and dust
twenty-five thousand years before she had been born.

They had run beyond the sight and sound of that mating-place, and
then, at the over-quickening of Clair's breathing, the hunter had slowed
down and looked at her inquiringly. They were in a treeless stretch of
long grass, the river deserting them and holding southward.

Across the grass, a mile or more away, two great hairy beasts shoggled through the afternoon, one after the other. Wooly rhinoceros. Clair, panting, had brought her eyes back to Aerte.

They had smiled together. Clair had thought: "And where from here?"

He had answered that by taking her hand again and breaking again into the trot that was probably his customary pace. The trees drew nearer. Clair saw that they were beeches, with great open spaces between. The rhinoceros had disappeared. Clair, breathing desperately, lay down. Aerte halted, laughed, gestured. Then he laid the spear down beside her and vanished among the beeches.

When she had recovered her breath she heard the sound of him returning and saw what he carried. It was a great watermelon. She sat up, looking at him lightedly. His grave eyes laughed down at her.

She had reached up and kissed the Cro-Magnard's lips. . . .

Where would the night find them and their companions? Back in the caves?

Aerte had shaken his head when they stood on their feet again and she gestured that question.

He said: "Over the hills."

They had perhaps half a score of words between them, as they went across the sunset land.

At length they drew nearer to the hills—great redstone masses unusual enough in the Atlantean scene. Gorse in thickets climbed their flanks. Birds rose whirring at their approach. Plover. It grew cold.

She became aware that they were threading in single file a long cleft in the hills. Golden flanked as the hills, Aerte led the way.

Beyond the winding cleft, she realized they had swung northeastward. Across the savanna waste, remote, towered the plateau where she had journeyed from the wreck of *Magellan's Cloud*. A week ago!

There lay the lake in the dying light. Perhaps if they listened they would hear that lowing again. She had caught the hunter's arm then and stayed him, listening. But from the dimming plateau-world and its foreground had come no sound other than a faint rustle.

They climbed. The lake receded, blurred, vanished. And at length, on a bush-strewn ledge, Aerte had drawn aside a bush and shown their shelter for the night. She understood then the reason for his disappearance the day before. Some twelve to fourteen feet deep, the shelter, though not more than four feet high.

Round the walls were things that looked to Clair like paintings, but the light went then and she could make nothing of them. The hunter motioned her inside. He was standing against the sunset. It was very still. She heard the beating of his heart and thought that were the light clearer she might verily see that beating. . . .

Man. Aerte. One and the same, here in the night that was the morning
of the world. And if she closed her eyes for a moment she would see
him hanging in the barb-wire entanglements of Mametz trench.

She had called him in then startledly, her face quivering, and he had
come, and ceased to have any symbolical significance whatever, and had
been merely the strange dark hunter, and, of course, the mate.

As they sat again in the twilight, later, her arm was round the bare
shoulder of the hunter. She told him in a slow murmur of words of which
he had no understanding, and he had understood and brought from the
back of the cavelet cooked fish, several of them, wrapped in great leaves.
She sat and ate with great appetite, wiping her fingers in the grass, and
reflecting on the amount of germs she must be eating. . . .

She had said of the hunter and the others, that they were children,
and so they were. She was twenty thousand years older than he—than
these others around them. Behind her marched the blood ghosts of all
history; behind the ancestry of this golden boy beside her was nothing
but long millennia of vivid harmless lives, reaching back to the time
when men were not yet men. . . .

CHAPTER NINE—*Sir John: His Prophecy*

IT DID not rain the next day, nor the next. Instead, they burned with
the vivid radiance of a Mediterranean summer; they burned their
sights and sounds into the soul of Clair Stranlay. Each evening found
her back in the painted cavelet—and aurochs stood in challenging regard
of a chrome-red lion in that cave—but nights and evenings were only so
many jade beads on the golden garments of the suntime hours.

Clair in those hours discovered the wonder of the earth itself—as
though it were a thing apart from her, yet no more apart than grass and
trees and that aurochs' calling and the cry of a wounded deer. She went
out into mornings that changed from dull gray to amethystine clarity
and a hold-your-breath silence, from that to a nameless stir and scurry
and beat that brought the sun orange and tremendous above the Atlantean hills, pringling with warmth on chilled back and face. These, and
the smell of the smoke from the fire kindled in the bright weather and
drifting blue wavelets across the face of the hunter. Noon, and lying in
sunlight in a sunlight dream, drinking in that sun, and the smell of the
crushed grass under her head.

But the second nightfall a troubled brooding look came into the grave
eyes of Aerte. He turned at the mouth of their shelter and pointed toward

the plateau that with each falling of dust kindled its volcano-torches to watchful brightness. He gestured ineffectively. He and Clair looked at each other dumbly in the dusk. Something—

And next morning they went out from the painted cavelet of sixty hours' residence, and Clair never saw it again. For that morning the band went west before the sun, slowly, in no great hurry, yet with intention.

Once they stopped to bathe in a lagoon from which they were evicted by the splashings and blowing of a great beast such as Clair had never seen before—a thing with a body like an unfortunate bee-vat, four stumpy legs, a hide that seemed to suffer from mildew and a head that was a bewildering confusion of teeth, tusks, horns and bosses. It splashed and paused and pawed, watching the bathers, and Clair felt the hunter tug at her hair. She turned, treading water, and followed him. Nor any too soon, for the multihorned animal at that moment charged them from the bank with the speed of an express train.

Clair it missed by inches, but they were as good as so many miles, for the beast's speed carried it into deep water where it floundered and squawked piercingly, evidently unable to swim. Its musk odor lay like a scum upon the water. Eying it, the hunter hefted his spear thoughtfully, and then shook a regretful head as it gained a sand-bank and stood blowing and dripping there.

"I'd sooner eat a goods-wagon," Clair told him.

She told him many a thing as unintelligible. She found it a saving necessity to keep herself in remembrance that a week before she had been Clair Stranlay, not a wanderer with a savage through a land lost in the deeps of time. A savage! At that her laughter went up to the soaring circus of carrion birds gathered in haste to watch the shoreward meanderings of the ill-tempered monster.

And suddenly, in the aurulent loveliness of the day, Clair felt sick with a strange queer dread of what the future might bring.

SINCLAIR saw their home-coming in the late afternoon of that third day. Sitting a little beyond and above the cave-mouths, peeling a long wand and binding either end of that wand with deer-gut, he saw them come. He paused at work.

Clair Stranlay!

(Ten days before: *Magellan's Cloud;* a languid loveliness in an expensive frock, with painted lips and ironic, inquiring gaze. . . .)

Safe they seemed. They came over the hills, the hunter pony-laden, Clair carrying the spear. In the blaze of the sun setting she saw the American and waved the old Stone Age spear. He waved in reply and then returned to work on the peeled wand.

They splashed through the river, stopping midway, the hunter to lave himself from head to foot, for he was very warm, having killed the pony on the run only a few minutes before. Sinclair descended from his ledge.

"Hello, Keith!"

"Hello, Clair."

She found his stare impossible to meet. A slow wave of color ebbed into her cheeks. She thought: "I *will* look at him," and look at him she did, resolutely, then.

"Sight of him with you makes me realize more than anything else the damnable impossibility of it all. Where did you go?"

She told him something of the two days. A boy came wandering out of the caves, saw her, gave a hail of welcome that brought out Zumarr and others. She stood in the midst of a laughing friendly throng, unalien to them, as Sinclair realized, as she had never been to her own century.

Darkness was very near. Now the radiance from the cave fires stole out across sedge and savanna in pursuit of the hasting daylight.

Returned, the hunters were singing in unison.

"WHAT are they singing?" he heard an English voice. He found Clair alone with him again. The others had drifted back to the caves to join in that song.

"Singing? I suppose it is a song about killing a horse."

"Filthy business. I helped Aerte to kill one."

"You helped at the same business before you met him. Remember that little deer up on the plateau?"

Clair remembered. "And we thought we were in West Africa. Instead—"

The instead was beyond speech. Sinclair looked across the river. He said, abruptly:

"Listen, Miss Stranlay, we're here by such kind of accident as probably never happened before. Twenty-five thousand years or more before the birth of Christ. It means hardly anything saying those words; but they have meaning.

"We're here, members of a tribal group that, for all we know, are the only human beings yet on earth. Certainly it's ancestral of the Cro-Magnards and half the modern population of Europe. And there is no Europe yet, there is no modern population." He spoke very slowly.

"This is the Golden Age of the human race. I don't know how long it will be before the Fourth Glacial time. Perhaps three thousand years.

But it's coming, and by then the descendants of those people—the descendants of your children—will have drifted across to the fringes of Europe. Through thousands and thousands of years they'll drift with all the chances of famine and starvation and mauling and killing by beasts that are Nature's chances, and may be shared by your children and their children, and endured because of the things between that will be like the happiness in the lives of these present hunters—like those two days you've spent with the hunter Aerte. But this life does not last for ever.

"In the Nile Valley, four thousand years before the birth of Christ, an accident is to transform the human race and human nature. Do you know that there will be descendants of yours whom they'll stretch out on sacrificial altars—babies of yours—and rip their hearts out of their chests? Do you know your descendents will be tortured in dungeons, massacred in captured cities, devoured at cannibal banquets?

"In Tyre they'll burn alive those children of yours inside the iron belly of Baal. Rome will crucify them in scores along the Appian Way. They'll chop off their hands in hundreds when Vercingetorix surrenders to Caesar. Can't you hear mounting down through the years the cry of agony from those children of yours that may so easily be? I can. I can close my eyes and hear the dripping of their blood."

So could Clair. "I never thought of that. Oh . . . horrible and terrible!" She covered her face. "Why did you tell me? Perhaps—*perhaps there were babies of mine who died on the barb-wire there in France, who are starving in the London streets now, drowned in some awful Welsh mine. . . .*"

He did not move. He said to her, as she stood weeping: "Fantastic stuff we are, Miss Stranlay! Not you and I only. All the human adventure. . . . Here, on an autumn night in Atlantis. On the edge of an adventure that probably no other thing in the cosmos will ever attempt. . . ." He paused. "By God, if we should ever get back!"

"Back?"

He laughed. "I still can't forget, still can't realize that this is reality for us. Of course there's no going back."

He stood beside her, silent. There came a drift of laughter from the caves. It was as though they stood, an old man and woman, outside a children's playground. And then Clair touched Sinclair's arm.

"I'd forgotten. Where is Sir John?"

SIR JOHN MULLAGHAN lay wrapped in a long dark skin that might have been a dyed sheepskin but for the fact that there were no sheep in the world where he lay dying.

His face, grimed and hirsute, as though it were the face of the one-time armaments manufacturer dead and dried and smoked in some head-hunter's hut, looked up at her and then suddenly shriveled and then grew bloated in one of the spasms of pain that were unceasing.

The odor of that corner of the cave was horrible. But Clair knelt unhorrified. The din of the golden communal life was stilled about them—strange thing this prehistoric foreshadowing of long sick-room silences round many a bed of pain through many a thousand years!

"I'm glad you're back safely, Miss Stranlay. Nice honeymoon?"

She smiled down at him unsteadily. "Lovely."

"That's good." His gray head moved dimly, the words came staccato, as by an effort. "Unfriendly—if I'd gone—without waiting for your return."

"You're not going. It's just difference of food, Keith says. We'll hunt up berries and green stuff for you to eat. You'll be well as ever in a day or so."

"Sinclair didn't say that, I fear. I'm poisoned and can't eat anything." She saw the ghost of a smile. "Nature didn't design me for a caveman. I'm afraid. . . . You've come back in time. There is the rain again."

So it was. Thunderously. Suddenly, beyond the cave-rims, the cup of darkness cracked. Lightning played and shimmered in the interstices, filling the cave with echoes. Then the darkness closed again. Clair saw Sinclair standing beside them, kneeling beside them.

"Drink this, Mullaghan."

"What is it?"

"Herb broth. I found a hollow stone and have had it cooking the last two hours."

The gray head moved upward painfully. Clair looked away. Then:

"Sorry, Sinclair, I'm afraid I can't."

"All right. Don't worry. I'll bring some water."

For a full minute after the American had gone he lay so silent that Clair thought he had fallen asleep. But he moved, again in pain. He chuckled, unexpectedly, surprisingly.

"The head of the League of Militant Pacifists acting as sick-nurse to an armaments manufacturer!"

"I'll help him now I'm back."

He spoke, but did not seem to answer her. "And Clair Stranlay, the novelist. But there are fine things in her, I think, though her books are the nonsense of the half-educated.

"Courage and honesty and a happy pessimism. . . . Her books? They are just such desperate, half-articulate, half-unconscious protestings as

Sinclair's threats of sabotage and assassination. . . . The savages of civilization. . . .

" 'Savages!' My God, Merton, the fantastic nonsense we have been taught! I lived in the midst of a paleolithic tribe twenty-five thousand years ago. Heroes and kindly women, kindly children all of them. And you have spent your life blackening the memory of them in your lectures and classes—and I have spent mine in murdering their descendants.

"I didn't *know*. . . ."

He said in a whisper: "We murdered her sweetheart—a boy—on the barb-wire outside Mametz. She told me. That was why she went away with the hunter that afternoon. Lost somewhere in the Atlantis hills. . . ."

The night wore on.

Sinclair came and went continuously, with water which he boiled above the far bright fire by the near entrance. Once he said to Clair:

"You can't do anything. You had better go and lie down."

"Not until he sleeps."

"Mr. Speaker, in moving support of this bill for disarmament by example, I am aware that I am both contradicting previous utterances of my own and taking a line of action in direct opposition to that pursued by the great party to which I belong, and to my own private interests. But I plead for my former attitude an ignorance of the essential nature of man as crass as any member of this House may ever have confessed to.

"I lived the scientific delusions of my age—strengthened as these delusions were by the act of a stray madman which brought a very bitter tragedy into my own life. . . . But the wreck of the airship, of *Magellan's Cloud* on the ancient continent of Atlantis, and my experiences there in company with two other survivors, among primitive men who were our own ancestors—literally, sir, opened my eyes.

"I found no 'howling primordial beast'; I saw nothing to indicate that man is by nature a cruel and bloodthirsty animal. It became plain to me that the vicious combativeness of civilized man is no survival from an earlier epoch: it is a thing resultant on the torturing dreads of civilization itself. . . ."

The sound of the rain! Clair heard it rise gustily and drown in momentary volume of sound the speech that Sir John Mullaghan, remote in space and time, was delivering to the English House of Commons.

THIS adventure in pre-history! As if any woman whatever who had loved a man and been by him loved, did not know the true nature of the kindly child immortal, though cult and environment twisted his mind and instincts, though press and pulpit shouted that he was by nature a battling animal, a sin- and cruelty-laden monster!

She started drowsily, sleep pressing on her eyelids. Sir John talking or herself thinking? She heard him then, his voice clear and sharp:

"Gentlemen, we must transform our factories to other purposes. There are still bridges to be built and tunnels to be excavated. Flying-machines. . . . We have barely glimpsed the universe in which man adventures, yet you and I have sat in this room and planned murder and destruction and called it business and patriotism. . . ."

Sinclair came tiredly through the red-ochered murk at that moment, and again held water to dim lips. All the cave was as some gigantic Arcadian sarcophagus: it seemed to Clair, as once before, that it was a place of the long-dead in which she knelt, and overhead washed the Atlantic. . . . Sir John said, very distinctly:

"Miss Stranlay—I thought she was here?"

"So she is. Here she is."

He peered up at them, his eyes very bright. "I've been dreaming—that next war. You two—promise me you'll get back, and tell them!"

"We'll get back," Sinclair said steadily.

"You must get back. They're planning it again. . . . Tell them, Sinclair. Fight them even with your bombs if they won't listen. . . . They *shall* listen. For there was hope even in that age out of which we came—more hope than ever before since civilization began. Else we could never have dreamed this dream, we three who are its children. The slayer and the soldier pass and Man will walk the earth again. . . ."

Clair felt the American's hand on her shoulder in the ensuing silence. He gave a sigh of relief.

"He's sleeping now. We can take it easy. If you're as dead-beat as I am—Hell, what was that?"

CHAPTER TEN—*Exodus*

IT WAS as though a great beast stirred in dreams under the floor of the cave. Clair was instantly on her feet beside the American. She saw it was close to dawn: the river glimmered beyond the fires. The watcher of the fires himself squatted not far away, nodding, undisturbed, though the faintest rustle of a nearing beast would have roused him to instant activity.

Clair whispered, "What was it?"

"Remember back beside the lake? Some kind of earthquake shock. . . . Here it is again."

The cave rocked. They held to each other for a moment. The shock
passed. Clair peered past the drowsy fire-watcher. "These people must
be used to it. None of them has wakened."

Not a hunter or a woman had stirred. They lay and slept in healthy
disregard of the earth's freakish moods. The fires burned low, yet glowed
enough to show the painted uintatherium still bunched with head etern-
ally lowered. Funny to think that that beast ("at this moment!") in the
twentieth century might still survive in this cave long sunk two miles or
more below the level of the ocean! . . . The thought made Clair whisper
another question:

"Wasn't this continent sunk in an earthquake?"

She saw a pallid flicker of a smile on Sinclair's face. "*Will* be. . . .
Let's see if anything's happening outside."

The fire-tender nodded to them. They paused at the cave-entrance and
looked out. Nothing. The rain had cleared away. The sky was pallid with
the waning lights of the stars awaiting the morning. The crispness of the
air caught at their throats. But there was also an unusual quality.

"Sulphur," said Sinclair. "Stay here. I'm going out to look."

He vanished, tall and white, into that waiting unease of the morning.
Clair thought: "Dictatorial still. But a dear."

She became aware of a pillared whiteness, like Lot's wife, against
the grayness of the morning. It was Sinclair, beckoning.

The grass was wet and cold. The morning wind blew chill on them
as they passed together outside the farthest flow of the cave-fires' radiance
and climbed over the smooth back of the bluff. And, as they did so, the
smell of sulphur increased with every step they took. Nearing the top
of the bluff, Clair, looking upward, suffered a curious optical illusion.
It seemed to her that the grass on the knoll, that the whole summit, was
lighted to an unwonted glow, as though a great fire were kindled on the
other side. But, the summit attained, she saw she had suffered from no
delusion. She gasped and stared.

IN THAT hour they should have seen but a little way across the jumble
of foot-hills and nullahs toward the mountain land which they had
descended a short week before. Instead, all that landscape which should
have lain in morning darkness was lighted uneasily, a welter of unstable
candle-points of flame, and backgrounding it, mile on mile, from one
end of the horizon to the other, was a dark-red glow that glimmered and
faded and grew to purple being and then died again, yet never quite, like
a fire that lives in a half-charred stick.

Momentarily, as they watched, the red and ocher faded from the glow,

yet that was through no waning of its strength, as they saw, but with the
coming of the morning. And with that coming the mystery grew plainer:
The whole of the dim mountain land of their first adventures had vanished into some fissure of the earth from which now arose the corona
of its destruction.

Twenty miles away to the north the vivid line of flame stalked the
horizon, and in the nearer distance they saw a pale advancing gleam.

"Floods—it's the sea!" said Clair.

Sinclair peered forward from beneath his hands. "Hell, and it is!
We'll have to run for it."

But he did not. He said, a second later: "It's advancing no longer.
Only through the light growing it seems to be. The floods have stopped."

So it seemed, now. Daylight was almost upon the land, and the havoc
of fire and water grew clearer. The sea had come far in—in places it was
not more than two or three miles distant. More than that. They stood
now on what was a great promontory, for this was higher land than to
east and west. And, advancing out of the water-threatened valleys were
long trains of moving objects that ran and squealed and jostled.

"Trek of the animals," said Sinclair. "Look—the mammoths!"

A great herd of them led the exodus. They came at racing speed,
great tusks uplifted, trunks uplifted, untrumpeting, with flying coats of
dun-red hair. They thundered past not half a mile away. Then Clair
saw her first aurochs, also running in herds, the gigantic beasts whose
lowing she had listened to many a time since that first night by the lake.

Horned and maddened, with belching breaths of spume they ran,
swinging round the corner of the bluff so that Sinclair, seeing the danger
there might be to the cave-dwellers below, turned and ran down the hill,
calling to Clair stay where she was. Safest place. . . .

The hills drummed with flying hoofs. Great deer, and Irish elk, a pack
of lions like loping St. Bernards, here and there a trundling bear. Then
herd on herd of ponies, with manes in quivering serration. The day
brightened, and with its brightening the glow in the north abruptly
flickered and vanished. The pulsing flight of beasts thinned, but the birds
still passed overhead in great flocks, tern and snipe and partridges either
momentarily startled or out on definite migration.

Up till then no animal had attempted the scaling of the bluff, but now
two leopards did so. Sly and suave, they came in loping bounds, not
greatly frightened, evidently, though in flight. One had been swimming,
and the water glistened on its sleek black coat. They slithered leftward
at sight of the kneeling woman. Then one crouched and snarled—

The charge of the brute rolled her on the ground. It had charged, not leaped, being over-hungry, and had hit her with its shoulder, instead of pinning her to the earth. Its body sprawled across her, furry and musk and smelling vilely. She thought vividly. "My throat!" and screamed, and saw the other leopard looking away, with pricked ears. She caught the wurring muzzle of the brute above her. Screamed again. She was dragged to her feet by Aerte. She laughed hysterically.

All over in a minute. Three of the hunters, Aerte included, had seen the leopards and raced them up the opposite side of the hill. She saw Sinclair ascending more slowly, now that she was safe.

When Sinclair came up she was still trembling.

"Goodness—I—I always did hate cats. Never bathe. . . . Silly to shake, but I can't stop it. I think I'll go down to Sir John."

Sinclair looked at her apathetically; sat down. She was safe; the caves were safe. He felt he wanted to sleep for a month.

"Sir John is dead," he said tiredly.

THE sun lay brave on the hillside. The day marched bannered across the Atlantean sky. Little clouds tinged with purple went sailing by, free and very fleecy and lovely. More of the bird-flocks came from the north, holding into dim southern regions of the Pleistocene earth. Far below, in the open spaces between the caves and the river, the Cro-Magnards cut up the meat which had come, alive and maddened, past their doors in such abundance.

And on the hill-brow Clair and Sinclair watched the passing of the day. Clair sat resting and thinking, and yet trying not to think.

"But it can't be! He can't have died. We don't belong here; it couldn't have happened this way in time! Else he was dead long before he was born. This would have happened to him before we knew him. Before the *Magellan* was wrecked he was dead." She giggled a little bit. "We've been talking to a corpse all this last fortnight."

Sinclair said nothing bleakly. Clair, exhausted, dozed. Later, she felt a hand on her shoulder, and aroused to Sinclair speaking at last.

"I won't leave you long. Shout if anything comes near."

"Where are you going?"

But he had gone. She sat, clasping her knees, sun-warmed, earth-kissed, vividly aware of the beauty and pleasure of her self. And below, in the Cro-Magnard caves, was that other body, finished with this and the sun and the rain and the hearing of laughter forever. Impossibly dead in an impossible country in an impossible epoch.

She looked back over the bluff. Sinclair and two hunters, burdened, were coming up. A few feet from Clair they halted. One of the hunters was Aerte.

They lowered something to the ground.

Next instant she found Aerte beside her. He put his arms around her. He laughed gravely and pointed down to the river in the sunlight. His brows knitted puzzledly as she shook her head and indicated the body wrapped in the pelt from the cave. He glanced at it indifferently, smiled again and tried to pull her to her feet. She shook him off; his touch was suddenly as shuddersomely repulsive as that of an unclean animal.

"Keith—*send him away.*"

She did not look round again as the American spoke to the two hunters, but she heard the sound of a lingering, puzzled retreat through the low brittle grass. Then the noise of Sinclair digging with a hand-ax. At that she rose and went and helped him. They worked in silence.

"Stand away, Miss Stranlay."

She stood aside and looked down over the flood-sodden lands. Already the darkness waited for them. She heard Sinclair dragging the body to the shallow pit. Then a sound of scraping and the fall of earth. Sinclair said: "Throw some earth, Miss Stranlay."

She turned round, seeing the grave almost completed. She picked up a handful of clayed dust and dropped it through her fingers. Sinclair replaced the turf and walked over it, stamping it gently.

Then he held out his hand to Clair and she went to him.

IT SEEMED to her that something had numbed her body and brain alike, through and through, in the next twenty-four hours. The second nightfall Sinclair came and sat down beside the fire of Zumarr, who glanced at him questioningly and from him toward another fire at which the hunter Aerte had again taken up quarters, as in times before the Mating for the Dark Days.

"Clair."

She roused a little. "Oh, it's you, Keith."

He stretched himself out beside her. His square dark head was oddly similar to Zumarr's. She thought, apathetically, "They might be brother and sister." He put a twig on the fire. Abruptly he said:

"This can't go on, you know."

She said dully: "What?"

He seemed to be considering his answer. Then:

"These people aren't to blame, Clair, but you. I mean your hunter and the others when they thought Mullaghan's death and dead body of no account. Neither, really, were they. Death is of no account in fundamental human values—the things these people live by. Your hunter saw a man lying dead—one to whom he had never talked, a puzzling stranger, a man who had presumably lived to the full, and was now dead, as was the order of things.

"And if your hunter thought about it at all, it was simply that he himself would also die some time, but meantime there was living to be done—eating, and marrying with you, and painting his pictures, and hunting, and every moment in which to live his body before he also was dead. That was all. It was perfectly natural."

"I know. And it has made me sick and frozen."

"It has no cause to make you any such things. If he'd seen Sir John lying ill or wounded he'd have carried him miles to safety. You know he would. They are absolutely unselfish and absolutely natural. Nothing horrible in death to them; there *is* nothing horrible in death.

"It is merely that you and I are laden down with the knowledge of that past that is not yet—with all the dismal funeral rites in our memory and that ritual of sorrow that isn't natural at all, but was an artificial thing foisted on human nature in a matter of mistaken science. It is these people who are clean and you who are diseased."

"I know," Clair said again. "Oh, Sinclair, I'll go mad, I know I will. Natural and clean? Of course they are. Splendid and shining and lovely, all of them. Aerte—he's my husband. . . . And they're not kin to me at all. I'm not human if they are. I'm the diseased animal, and it's not the winter or the memory of Sir John that'll kill me. It's realization of a fact. I can't go on with it, I can't!"

"You filthy little weakling."

He said it in an even voice.

"You little gutter-snipe of the London slums! I thought you had guts in you. You haven't. You've a pious rotten romanticism that's no relation to reality. Think I don't know—that I haven't watched your antics ever since I was fool enough to drag you out of the *Magellan?* And I was a fool; I fooled myself about you. Here, especially.

"I thought this place and these people had done to you what they did to me and poor Mullaghan—discovered the human in you. But there wasn't a human to discover."

Clair shook herself and leaned forward to the fire and also put a twig on it. Then she laughed, and, looking at Sinclair, shook her head.

"Thanks. But it's really not necessary."

He flushed, suddenly, darkly. "I thought it might work."

"It has, in a way." She raised her head and looked across the cave toward Aerte's fire. "Goodness. . . . Sorry I've been all you said."

"You haven't, of course. . . . But I need help as well, Clair. All this

stuff I talked—about the naturalness of regarding death casually—I know
as well as you do that it's impossible for us, just as it's impossible for
us ever to live the lives of these hunters. I know that wall of glass as
well. . . . But Mullaghan's gone, and if you went and I were left on my
own—I also don't want to go mad. . . ."

CLAIR said soberly: "I'm both sick and sorry. Oh, I'm damnably
selfish." She held out her hand. "I don't think we've ever been
friends. Can't we be?"

He held her hand a moment. "This is the last night in these caves."

She was startled. "Why?"

"You haven't heard, of course. They've left you alone, thinking
you're sick. But the exodus was decided on this afternoon. There's no
game anywhere in flooded country round about, nor anywhere to the
south as far as the hunters have penetrated. That earthquake and the
sinking of the mountain land have left this section a deserted peninsula.
The cave is going to be abandoned tomorrow."

"And where are they going?"

"Southward, somewhere, in pursuit of the game. And it's not only
threat of famine, of course. You haven't noticed, not being outside the
cave. But there was frost this morning; the new lagoons, half salt at that,
were covered with ice. It'll be a winter of such terrors as these people
have never endured—at least as far north as this."

Clair looked at the painted animals overhead. "And they're to leave."
It seemed that she had lived in these caverns for months. "We knew that
this happened in pre-history—or will happen. . . . Goodness, tenses do get
mixed in the time-spirals. . . . Is this the coming of the Ice Age?"

"I don't think so. It's just that Atlantis is the most unstable of the
continents. That, of course, we know from the future out of which
we've come. It's doomed."

"And these people?"

"They're the ancestors of the Cro-Magnards from Cro-Magnon in
France, remember. So some of them at least are to push eastward, and
some years or generations hence strike Europe."

"Isn't it bound to happen, then?"

"Not necessarily. Perhaps the future we came from was one of many
possible futures—"

"I thought that—once—but I'd forgotten."

"There was nothing fixed and real about that twentieth century of
ours, Clair. Civilization as we knew it—it has still to happen. Perhaps it
need never happen. Perhaps we can prevent it, sabotage it in advance—

"There is no need for the processes of history, as we know them, ever to take place. You and I can alter the very beginnings. Listen: We're going south, and it will get warmer. Somewhere beyond the southward mountains we saw from the plateau these people will find new hunting-grounds. Then you and I can get to work. We can teach them the beginnings of civilization without any of civilization's attendant horrors."

"What, for example? I'm horribly ignorant."

He shook his head. "It's just that you don't realize what you know. Pitchers—they've never thought of using gourds to store water at night. That for a beginning. Then in hunting: I'm engaged in making a bow. But these are the lesser things. Somewhere beyond those southward mountains we'll find a river and wild millet or barley or corn. We can start the first agriculture—plowing and seeding will be simple enough. That for next spring. And in the summer get them to build a corral and drive wild cattle into it; they can tame them in a few years.

"Next autumn take a party prospecting in the mountains—I know something about metals. . . . Flax or hemp growing, perhaps. Even with crude metal implements and rough fiber bandagings I could save half the women who die in childbirth. And iodine and such-like are easy enough extracts. . . . We can leap twenty thousand years and take these people with us if we plan it carefully. Preserve this sane equality that's theirs, take care that no idea of gods or kings or devils ever arises in their minds. We can transform humanity."

CLAIR began to kindle to his words. If they could! "But—aren't the cruelties and the taboos bound to rise with civilization? Better to leave our hunters alone for the Golden Age that is still theirs than try and fail."

"We won't fail. Much better to leave them if there was any chance of failure. If there were no choice for the future but history as we know it, a thing inevitable awaiting these people, it would be better for them and for the world if we poisoned them or drove them to starvation.

"But there's no reason why we should fail. The foul things of civilization were an accident. . . . Time and history will go on long after we're dead here in Atlantis, Clair, but there need never be a pyramid built or a city massacred or a war or a miners' strike. We can remake the world."

"Goodness, we will! . . . Keith, there's Gloezel!"

"Eh?"

"Don't you remember reading about it a few years back? That place in France where heaps of Neolithic relics were dug up, and were said to be fakes because they were mixed with modern-looking bottles and jars and the scratchings of a primitive alphabet? . . . Perhaps this experiment we're going to try was known to us already in that twentieth century from which we came! Perhaps Gloezel saw the end of this plan of yours, and men of those days forgot your teachings, and the civilizations and the savageries rose in spite of the dream we brought these hunters."

Sinclair laughed and stood up. "Perhaps there have been other voyagers into time than you and I. Perhaps time and history can not be altered. Yet if they can—"

Somewhere in the depths of the caves a sick child was crying. He stood and listened to it and then looked down in Clair's fire-bright face.

"There need never be a lost baby crying again in the world that we can make."

And next day the Cro-Magnards of that nameless valley in Atlantis left the fires in the painted caves still burning, and gathered their children and their implements and the skins of the beasts they had killed in generations of hunting, and forded the river, and turned to the south.

The rain cleared, and a cold sun shone, and far in the north the new lakes shivered in a brisk wind. They passed through a deserted country, with not even birds in it. They passed out of the Atlantean valley as dream-people pass from a dream dreamed by a drowsy fire. Coming from the east or west hundreds of years before, their ancestors, descendants of the dawn-men who lived in Java and Peking and the Sussex downs, had descended upon the valley, a place of good hunting, and settled there.

And the years had passed in the flow and ebb of death and love and birth, times of plenty and times of famine, with neither memory of the past nor fears of hopes for the future. The sun and the wind, the splendor of simple things, had been theirs: that Golden Age that was to live for ever, a wistful thing, in the minds of men.

Now they were out on an adventure that followed no road Clair Stranlay could fore-plot.

They carried their sick and their aged with them, and they went gayly enough, with laughter and singing, the young men stringing out far in advance across the southern savannas. They went in no great order, but a friendly southward drift. Alone perhaps of them all Clair and Sinclair stopped a little while and looked back.

"There will be fishes swimming in that cave years hence," said Clair. "Poor Mullaghan!"

And that was strange enough to think of also. Thousands of years away, perhaps preserved uncorrupted and incorruptible by the pressures of water and rock, the body of Sir John Mullaghan would lie in that grave they had dug for it with the flint spears of Cro-Magnard hunters.

The knoll glimmered.

"And now—" said Sinclair.

So they too turned about and went, their white faces strange phenomena still in the wake of the golden men of the dawn. The savannas rose green and brown and cobalt in the distance. Far and remote beyond these, many days' journeyings away, were the mountains where Sinclair planned to change the course of history.

Behind them, the winter followed on their tracks.

CHAPTER ELEVEN—*Clair Lost*

CLAIR STRANLAY was lost.

She looked back, shading her eyes with her hand against the pale afternoon sunlight, to the track she had taken across the withering grass to this eminence in the southern foot-hills. But all the country was desolate and deserted, except by a far loch where curlews called and called. Nothing moved or took to itself animate being in that still land. Up that track she had come. But before that?

She sat down to consider the matter. There was the forest. But which forest? The country was ribbed with just such masses of trees, and the rise and fall of nullahs confused all knowledge as to whether one mass was a separate entity or the winding continuation of another. . . .

"I'm shockingly hungry," said Clair aloud.

The silent countryside took no notice. Clair pushed her hair from her eyes and stood up again. It would be nonsensical to rest now. Somewhere, from higher up, she would be bound to see the hunters or the encampment.

She climbed through grass that was sedgy because of a trickle of water from the hillside. A ridge, like the scales on the back of a stegosaurus, ran along its summit. Here the grass gave place to lichened rock—granite rock, she noted, and red granite at that.

The red slivers cut her feet, hardened though these had grown. But at last, though with some difficulty, she attained a platform-ledge that dominated all the hill and indeed all the country. Panting, she looked again into the north.

Made miniature in distance, the land was otherwise unchanged. No sign of the Cro-Magnards or their encampment anywhere.

If she made a fire—?

Realization of a startling fact chilled her a little. She had nothing with which to make a fire. She glanced down at the short-bladed flint spear in her hand. Flint. But no iron pyrite. The hunters used tinder and a drum-stick—things she was incapable of operating. No chance of raising a fire. Must watch for one instead.

For how long? She looked at the sun. Perhaps three hours more of daylight. She turned round slowly, in a circle, looking about her. So, very suddenly, she became aware at last of the mountains of the south.

From her stance, and for the first time in the southward trek, she saw them uprise plainly. Not only so, but gigantic. They filled all the southern horizon with their tumbled shapes. Distant, Andean, some trick of refraction allowed her to see the sun filtering into immense canyons, splashing in the remote upland tarns, crowning each point with quicksilver. The significance of that last gleam dawned on her.

"Snow."

They were perhaps twenty miles away. Were they passable?

She thought: "Keith's plan to take the hunters south of them—he may never be able to carry it out. Necessary to try out our experiment on a southward river, protected by mountains in the north. . . . Wonder what he's doing now? Missed me? Sure to."

She had an afterthought, and smiled at it, absently. "And Aerte as well, I suppose."

How far away, both of them? Miles and miles, surely.

It was nine days since the beginning of their trek from the ancient cave. Acting on the apparently casual suggestion of Sinclair, the Cro-Magnards had held as directly southward as the nature of the country allowed. It was to them a matter of indifference what direction was taken, so long as game grew more plentiful. And certainly neither to left nor right was there that plentitude. But one colony of lions the general exodus of the animals had left behind, and on the fifth night of the trek these beasts, made bold by hunger, had raided the camp.

Clair and Sinclair had been awakened by the screams and shouts, and stirred to see a fire geyser under the impact of a lion landing from a misdirected spring. Clair had caught up a torch and thrust it into the face of one brute. Near her Zumarr had been killed and nearly disemboweled by the stroke of a huge paw. The fighting in the semi-darkness about the fires had gone on for many minutes. Then the lions had retreated, dragging several bodies with them. Devouring these, they had squatted all night in a semicircle beyond the fires, evidently determined not to abandon the neighborhood of this store of food which had descended on their famished land from the north.

Sinclair had gone about, binding up such wounds as grass and sinew seemed capable of salving. Aerte had come to Clair and crouched by her, looking toward the noise of the lions' grisly banqueting and gripping a spear in either hand. Then, toward the dawn, the Cro-Magnards had begun to move out toward the lions, discovering them replete and somnolent, all but two or three cubs which had had little share of the human meat. Out there, beyond the camp, a running fight began, until the morning came. Half a dozen or so of the lions escaped. The rest, dead, were skinned, and the Cro-Magnards cooked and ate meat from their haunches. Both Clair and Sinclair had refused it.

THROUGHOUT the next day and the next, holding south again, no game at all had been encountered. Food was growing very scarce, and the half-dozen lions, made cautious, but still hungry, followed up the trek, roaring at the night-time but venturing on no more raids.

But on the morning of this day on which Clair sat lost on the summit of her hill, a boy, slipping out of the camp in the early hours on some boyish foraging of his own, had wandered for several miles and then returned in a glow and much excitement.

The lions had vanished from about the camp, and he knew the reason. A herd of mammoth, many bulls and cows and three young ones, was gathered feeding near a stream and a hill.

The news had emptied the camp, at racing speed, of the golden men. Clair had caught up a flung spear and run by Sinclair's side, the spear a thrilling complement. "Though goodness only knows what for. Unless to tickle the mammoths. . . . What, for that matter, are any of us going to do with spears against them?"

"Aerte was telling me," Sinclair had said. "We'll drive one of the animals into the river and attack it there."

So they had done. One bull, perhaps the leader of the herd, had charged the yelling attack of the Cro-Magnards, a magnificent spectacle of wrath with uplifted trunk and threatening tusks. Him they had allowed to pass without casualty, and, once past, he had stood a moment meditating discretion or valor, and then taken to the open land and safety. The others, all but the selected two, had followed him.

Driving those twain into the river was the task.

Under the urge of a hail of stones one of them at length galumphed forward into the muddy embrace of the water and sank to the knees and was held there, like a fly in glue. And, as by so many hornets, hewing and stabbing, he had been instantly assailed. Not so the second. It had broken away to the right, trampling several hunters underfoot and impaling one on a great broken tusk.

Sinclair had taken abrupt command, his dour face flushed; perhaps the first commander in the world, for even in hunting parties the Cro-Magnards had no leaders. They were an orchestra without a conductor, yet a fairly efficient one at that, acting with a serene cooperativeness that suggested to Clair telepathy. But, under the direction of Sinclair's shout, such of them as had already attended the panicked antics of the second mammoth broke into two parties.

One raced for the hills, the other held in the track of the beast. Clair had joined the first group, and ran with them, feeling in a very glow of health, and had slipped and fallen; and had laughed and scrambled to her feet. Then she had found herself alone and lost.

As simply as that. For a time she had heard receding shoutings and once a wild trumpeting of agony that made her cover her ears. She had made in the direction of both sounds, as she believed. Neither could be more than half a mile distant. And no sign of hunters or hunted had met her eyes.

She had found herself in a series of low valleys, one fitting into the other with the suave necessity of shallow boxes in a Chinese puzzle. And when finally she had emerged from the labyrinth into open country again, it was a country of which she had no knowledge.

She had wandered the deserted Atlantean country since then, once stopping to drink at a pool, once finding a nest with three eggs in it, curious speckled eggs which she had broken and eaten raw, very thankful that they were fresh. Then she had hunted on again.

And this seemed the day's end of the hunt.

Bound to follow her. But could they? With a certain uncertainty gripping her she turned now from survey of the gigantic bastion in the south, and looked at the country out of which she had climbed. They had no dogs, they had no special scent themselves: scent was a later acquirement of specialized savages. She would have to wait until darkness and then look for the light of a fire somewhere down there. And food—

Beyond her hill, eastward, was another, and between the two of them a gleam of water. She realized the thirst parching her throat, and began to descend from the scaled back of the granite stegosaurus. The sun flung her a long shadow eastward as she walked, but it was only as she neared the hill and the water was near that she saw a mist was rising.

Between her and the distant nameless Andes the undulating, sparsely forested land was sheathed in an uneasy garment of damp wool. By the time she had knelt down and drunk and stood up again, the mist was all about her. She stood in uncertainty of it, walked a few steps, halted, determined to climb her hill again. But the hill had disappeared.

Now she walked along a rolling shoulder of earth that was either of the original eminence, or of that second hill she had seen in the east.

She came to another tarn. It reflected her face and body as her feet touched the edge. She leaned on her spear and looked down at herself.

A woman had come into the water and looked up at her gravely, from a heavy short-cut mane of brown hair with the red slightly bleached from it. But the red tints were still in eyes and brows.

So indeed her flesh was now tinted, yet in some fashion that left it none the less white. Leaving that reflection of herself to dream of her for ever, perhaps, in that lost pool, went on into a mist that presently cleared, like a curtain drawn aside, to disclose the splendors of the sunset on the Atlantean Alps.

With purple from the murex the sunset had garbed them, and with the red of rust, and a blue—an ultramarine blue that must have found its colors in those high glacial snows. . . . Clair had never seen such a sunset, and the stalking approach of darkness at her lower level was almost upon her before she noticed it.

With that darkness came a bitter coldness and a wind that seemed somehow dissociated from the cold, but cold itself. . . . And suddenly Clair knew that she was being tracked.

The beast had snuffled in a peculiar way. She wheeled round and saw nothing. Then—a hump of rock she had not noticed when she passed that way. It was not a hump of rock. The beast was crouching. There was not light enough for its eyes to gleam, she saw merely the dim shape, hunched, and the twitching of its ears. "Is it going to spring?"

She turned round and went on. The padding came on as well. This time she wheeled so rapidly that she saw the beast, not crouching this time, but on its feet, its ears still twitching.

And it was not a beast.

TO CLAIR it seemed that she stood and faced the thing through minute after minute of horror-struck silence. The spear was gripped and useless for the blood had deserted her hand. It grew momentarily darker, in wave on wave of lapping shadow from the sunset fire in the mountains of the south. And still Clair stood and stared wide-eyed at that hideous apparition out of pre-history.

It was a male, with the bigness of a gorilla and something of its form. It was hung with dun-red hair; crouched forward, its shoulders were an immense stretch of arching muscle and bone. Its gnarled hands almost touched the ground. It smelled. It stared at her filmily, and a panting breath of excitement came from its open jaws.

A Neanderthaler!

The thought flashed through her mind and was instantly disputed and dismissed. For the Thing had an immense bulge of forehead and no downward-pressing neck constriction such as she had read the lost race of Neanderthal possessed. Nor had it a single implement or weapon. It crouched, a strange, strayed, hungry, pitiful beast, looking at her.

What it was she did not know, was never to know, that member of some lost, discarded genus of sub-men that time was utterly to annihilate. Lost as herself she suddenly realized it was, and with that realization blood came back to her hand. She raised the spear and shouted, "Shoo!"

The Thing, half in sitting posture though it was, sprang back a full yard, and then, as Clair, desperately afraid, made at it, turned and shambled off in a rapid baboon-like scrabble. And as it went it uttered a strange moaning cry, growing louder and louder as the body behind the voice receded and finally vanished into the evening.

Clair, sobbing hysterically, no sooner saw it out of sight than she turned in her original direction and ran and ran, slipping and falling over rocks and once becoming desperately entangled in a soft and hairy bush which seemed to grasp at her with clammy hands. When finally she stopped, panting, there was no echo of that moaning ululation to be heard in the deserted hills, nor any sign of her stalker.

The running had warmed her, but now, stopping, she felt the wind drive against her icily. Some shelter she must have before the night came. And there was little chance in these hills, for they were of granite, not the familiar limestone so frequently honeycombed with caverns. Yet, in the thickening nightfall, she had not gone more than a dozen steps when fortune favored her and up the brow of the hill she saw an indentation. Attained with panting effort, she discovered it a fault of the strata that left a roofed, triangular recess some nine or ten feet deep, inadequate enough, but better than nothing.

She laid down her spear and ran to the foot of the hill where grass, sere and dry as hay, rustled and whispered eerily in that voiceless country. She tore up great armfuls of it and carried it up to the ledge. Meantime the force of the wind had increased, and as she made the last journey sleet began to pelt her body.

But the ledge was a heaped fuzz of hay. She ran inside, seized the flint spear, lay down on the hay and wound herself into the swaths, rolling over and over till the faintly burred heads had entangled her in a great coverlet from head to foot. The exertion had warmed her again faintly, but her whole body was still an icy numbness. When she finished and raised her head it was to see the blackness complete but for a strange

phenomenon. A white curtain wavered and shook in front of the ledge
of refuge. Hail.

She found she had forgotten hunger as she had forgotten to be afraid.
Yet the numbness of her body had not spread to her mind.

She thought of Aerte and that first night she had been with him in
the cave far to the north, watching the volcanoes burn in the land that
the seas were soon to devour. And instantly the memory passed from
her. Neither Aerte—his face seemed to take shape in the darkness and
then fade at once—nor that pitiful shade of Mametz seemed of im-
portance. She thought of Sinclair, and he passed from her mind, a dour
enigmatic ghost. Sir John Mullaghan—less than a ghost.

So with all she had ever known, all the tenants of the ancient world
of comfort and security. Only, in the sound of the bitter hail-storm that
thudded upon the hills, remained one piercing memory: the face of the
beast-man, lost and desperate as herself; astray in time and the world.

Had he found refuge or was he out in this? What a jest of God!
Millions and millions of years ago He had brought a warm fetid scum to
anchor on some intertidal beach. And it had fermented through long
nights and noons; and it was life. And life climbed and branched and
flowered from it. And the dragons passed and the mammals rose and
the great apes walked the hills of Siwalik. Westward they wandered,
through millennium on millennium, gathering their little skills with stick
and stone. And one by one God discarded them. For they bored Him.

Heidelberg man with the mighty skull, the ape-hunter of Piltdown, the
chattering beasts of Broken Hill and the Java jungles—they passed and
were not, bloody foam and spume on a sea that whimpered cruelty and
change. Till this Atlantean night of hail all these experimentings of
Nature's thousand millennia—they ended here in a nameless hill-land
with the ape-man and her, last representatives of kindred experiments.

She quivered to a misty drowsiness, even while a faint voice protested
through her frozen serenity, "But you are not the last!" Last she was.
Poor humanity, that had dreamed so much and so splendidly—to end
its dream with her! . . .

Thereon, warmed by the heat her body had engendered in the hay,
utterly exhausted with her day's marchings and searchings, Clair laid
her head on her hand and slept.

IT BEGAN to freeze as the night wore on. The cold grew more intense.
But it did not penetrate the grass coverings wherein Clair Stranlay
lay enwrapped. Not cold but cramped position made her awake, and,
shifting her aching hip, she saw that the hail had ceased and the moon-

light had come. It flooded all the uplands and came in little waves into the recess. She lay and looked out, suddenly vividly awake.

She thought: "You were hysterical, I suppose. The last woman in the world. . . Still, supposing Keith Sinclair is all wrong, and it's into the future we've strayed, not the past? Then this damn hunger of mine must be the accumulated hunger of centuries. . . . *Pâté-de-foie-gras* sandwiches. And spring lamb. And black coffee. And green chartreuse. And— you'd better not go on."

She wriggled a little, cautiously if light-headedly, toward the forepart of the cave. Now she could see the moonlit lands.

The silence of the strange day that had encompassed her wanderings was as nothing to this. Over a crisp white shroud that draped the countryside nothing moved or cried. Had she indeed dreamed? Was this not perhaps verily the end? Far below, to the right, a stretch of water gleamed icily, burnished and unrippled. Silence and the sweetness of death in the silence, beyond the water black armies of the trees.

And God? Was there indeed no God, were He and His variants no more than mistaken science—results of that seasonal ritual that grew in the Nile Valley when men ascribed the times of flood and ripening to the mysterious, animate sun? No more? And the Christ and the Buddha and their dream of a Father Who Knew if a sparrow fell? Were these no more than thin plaints of this lost adventure of mankind, crying for warmth and safety and comfort?

Was that God only the Anglicized version of the Nile-lands sun? A dream, Himself a hope and a terror as yet unborn, undreamed of here in the wastes of Atlantis or elsewhere in this world that awaited the coming of the last Ice Age?

Omnipotence and Omnipresence still unborn. Far up there in the stars God still lay unborn and unawakened. . . . Or dead, dead indeed if this were the last night of the world, swinging now a frozen star about an extinct sun.

"Then what am I? Why was I born to think these things? Oh, somewhere, surely, in some age to come, there's explanation. Of me and Sinclair and Sir John and the beast-man lost in these hills. . . ."

She covered her eyes from the bright moonlight. No sound, no answer came to her. None had ever come or ever would come.

And then Clair felt no longer afraid. She dropped her hands. She addressed the frozen world in a whisper.

"You lovely thing, you can kill me and finish me. Very easily. But not that question. It's beyond your killing. It'll live long after you're dead yourself."

IN THE morning she encountered and speared a half-frozen hare by the verge of the loch. Shuddering, she cut its throat and drank its blood. By night-fall she was far from the ledge where she had sheltered, holding across the savanna toward the southward mountains. Toward those mountains Sinclair was guiding the Cro-Magnards and somewhere on the verge of them she would overtake or intercept the trek.

The sun had risen, powerful and hot, and the thin frost-rime went fast from grass and forest. Clair ran as much and as often as she could, but many times had to sit and rub her numbed feet, agonizingly, back to circulation. No wind came across the hill-jumbled plain, and the southern peaks seemed to come but little closer with the passing of the day. Yet the hills where she had encountered the ape-man receded almost into flatness.

She made up her mind to perch in a tree during the night; so all day she kept near the winding forest-belts, lest darkness overtake her remote from the shelter she had determined on.

For shelter, cold apart, would be necessary. The land now swarmed with game. Once she came on a nest of hyaenodon, rolling and playing and snarling happily in the sun. They desisted at sight of her, and crouched with lolling tongues, looking at her quizzically. Two, hardly more than puppies, got up and cantered after her, falling over the grass-tussocks and their own legs foolishly.

Farther on she saw a herd of aurochs among the trees, and remembered the Latin tale of these animals having no knees and being unable to kneel or lie or sleep otherwise than unchancily poised against the bole of a tree. The Romans had been misinformed.

But in late afternoon the direct sunlight vanished, extinguished in a driving storm of snow, soft powdery stuff that felt almost warm at first, but speedily lost that quality. The landscape became a wavering scurry, as though the very savannas were seeking shelter. Clair turned into the safety of the trees, treading a great nave of pines with underfoot a thick carpet of needles which pricked her feet. Scotch firs grew here as well, and under one of them she crept and sheltered.

She could still see the land she had crossed, and, presently, in a late clearing of the snow-squall, a figure. A human figure.

She knew it a dream or a mirage and looked away, and rubbed her eyes, and looked back again. Then she started to her feet and found herself running toward him, calling and sobbing. He saw her, dropped his load and came running toward her eagerly and caught her in his arms.

"Aerte!" she cried.

It was Keith Sinclair.

CHAPTER TWELVE—A Light in the South

HE SAID breathlessly, "Clair! Are you all right?" And she could not answer because her head was pressed against his chest, and she was breathless with running and surprise, and felt she never wanted to speak again; only to hold him and hold to him and never let him go. So for a time they stood in each other's arms.

"You are Sinclair! I'm not the last left alive? Oh, Keith! . . ."

He turned away and picked up the bundle. It was a great bearskin. Beside it he had dropped a hunting spear and something else—a huge stringed bow that reached almost to his shoulder. He turned round to find Clair drying her eyes ineffectually. He saw her slim and brown-white and grimy, snow in her hair and goose-flesh across her shoulders.

"I thought I was lost for ever."

She darted forward and seized his spear and bow. "You dear to find me! I've got a tree to shelter under. Come along!"

The snow had begun again and they ran for the shelter of the forest. Under the Scotch fir no snow came, and only a waft of faint ice currents from the wind. Sinclair dropped his bundle and bent and untied it, not looking at her as he asked the question:

"Have you had any food?"

"I killed a hare this morning and drank its blood."

"And no fire? How did you pass the night?"

"Sheltering in a ledge up on the hills back there. I saw all the world lying dead last night, Keith."

He was gathering pine-needles and broken branches. He placed a little circle of rotten wood fragments round the heap and then fumbled in the bearskin. Some tarnished thing shone in his hand. Clair drew a long breath.

"Sir John's lighter. Does it still light?"

"He never used it after we came among the Cro-Magnards, you know. And the wadding is still a little damp with petrol—I hope." He flicked the lighter open. A tiny white-yellow flame kindled the wick. The wind had ebbed round and came from the north now. The flame ran swiftly along a twig. Clair, standing stared at it fascinatedly. A fire again! Sinclair put up a hand, and pulled her down.

"Sit here and don't let it go out. I'm going to erect a break-wind."

He bent and disappeared out of the sheltering circle of the fir-fronds, returning in a moment with an armful of boughs. He went back, foraging, and she heard him snapping-off others. Presently he was beside her again,

and began to construct the break-wind, interweaving from the ground
up to the fir-fronds a wall of boughs. Abruptly the wind ceased to blow
upon Clair's back. The fire changed from a sulky negligence to a gossipy
crackling. Sinclair lay beside her.

"That's that. God, I am glad to see you."

She saw then that he was utterly exhausted. His face was pinched and
dented with cold and other things, his eyes were bloodshot. Also, his
feet were so torn that the blood had splashed in long streaks up past
his ankles. She gave a cry at sight of them.

"They're all right." He was lying with closed eyes. "Stopped aching,
and the dirt in them's clean enough." He tried to rouse himself. "There's
pemmican in that parcel. Twine the bearskin round you. Keep up fire.
. . ." His voice trailed off into unintelligibility. She thought he had
fainted and leaned over him in some consternation.

He was asleep. Probably he had not slept all the previous night.

She undid the bundle and found inside it smoked meat, as he had
said, strange spongy stuff she had never seen before. Mammoth meat?
In the bundle was a package of stone-tipped arrows. Nothing else. She
cut off some of the meat with the blade of the spear which had com-
panied her, and mounted the spongy slices on arrow-heads, and crawled
out from below the tree to collect more fuel.

There, beyond the shelter of the breakwind, she realized the salvation
of Sinclair's coming. The snow had ceased again, but the wind was
almost a solid thing, and awful in its numbing coldness. Darkness was
driving across it, an opposing force, and she stumbled chilledly in
shadows, as she faced about to return to the fir.

There she found the meat smoking and Sinclair still fast asleep. She
flung the skin over him and tucked it about him, and he stirred a little
and muttered something; and she bent to hear what it was.

"Road to the south. She'll have taken the road to the mountains."

So he had guessed and followed on that chance? But a hazardous
enough guess, and when had he made it? Not until he had reached one
of those hills in which she herself had sheltered last night. That was
obvious. . . . Keith Sinclair! And she had thought—she had *known*
as she ran toward him—that he was Aerte.

Where were the hunters?

Useless questions. She thought, "Oh, it *is* good to eat," and ate the
meat slowly, carefully, wondering if she should awaken Sinclair to
share with her. But he was obviously more tired than hungry. The
saltless stuff in her mouth went over without effort nowadays. But a
drink—it might be impossible to find any water.

The break-wind had collected a drift of snow, and she gathered a
handful and ate it. She finished the sliver of meat in her hand, and
looked for the rest, and gave a little gasp. Oh, my good God, had she
eaten all that?

SHE piled more boughs on the fire. Now the wind was crying overhead.
The scotch fir drummed like a harp played on by a blind harper.
She found handfuls of damp leaves and cones and packed them about the
fire, their resinous smell homely in her nostrils. Then she crept over and
lay down, pulling a corner of the bearskin over her.

From there she raised her head and looked out from below the
whistling fronds of the tree, into the darkness of the forest and tundra, a
darkness based on a ghostly grayness that was the snow. She felt a
drowsy content upon her. She thought, withdrawing a chilled arm into
shelter, 'Goodness, how little we need for comfort!'

Her red-brown hair blew a little; she felt it rise and undulate pleasantly
on her head. She was about to lie down when something far away
caught her attention.

At first she thought it was a star and then realized the impossibility
of that. The night was too dense with storm-clouds. And, though it had
the twinkling immobility of a star, it was too low down there in the
horizon of the south. But it gleamed brightly, like a torch in an unsteady
hand, winking, as it seemed, across the leagues of tundra in the drive
of the same blizzard. What would it be?

Another volcano? But there had been no sign of a volcano during all
her southward tramp of the afternoon. The Atlantean Alps were great,
glacier-studded masses, not like that line of fires that had marched to the
right of the original trek of Sir John and Sinclair and herself from the
wreck of *Magellan's Cloud*. No volcano. It must be a fire.

But kindled by whom?

Staring across the night, a maze of drowsy speculations unfolded in
her brain. Other Cro-Magnards? But were there any, other than those
she knew? Perhaps—who knew!—another party of explorers from the
outer rims of Time, sucked into this epoch by just such accident as
wrecked the *Magellan's Cloud*. No impossibility. People perhaps out of
an age even remoter than the twentieth century. . . .

Still—perhaps simply a consignment from the same age and era as had
caught the *Magellan!*

The wind rose to a super-blizzard, and then fell and died. But all
through these hours, and into the pale coming of the next dawn, enigmatic, the fire in the southward mountains winked across the wastes.

THE American was the first to awake. The fire was out and the wind had died away and it was the beginning of daylight. He put aside the bearskin.

He remembered at once, and then, not moving, lay and looked at Clair who was still asleep.

He stood up and shivered in the waiting coldness of the morning. A moor-hen twittered. Water was not so far off. He stepped gingerly toward the fire and collected charred boughs, and scrunched around in search for Sir John's petrol lighter, and found it laid neatly at the base of the fir tree, in company with his bow.

His spear was nowhere to be seen, because at the moment Clair lay on it. He started a fire and then crept out from below the fir and held down through an avenue of pines to that twittering that told of the moor-hen's splashings. The sun came up over the eastward tundra at that moment and followed him. He found the water, a stream that meandered southward, and sat down on its snow-covered bank.

He was half-frozen already with his walking through that snow, but the cleansing of his feet at once was imperative. He set to work with handfuls of ice-cold water. Several times he felt he was about to faint in the spasms of agony. Clair's voice spoke behind him.

"Keith! Why didn't you ask me to help?"

He looked over his shoulder and saw her shivering behind him and carrying the bearskin. "Go back to the fire."

"Don't bully. We'll go when you're all right again. Sit on this and I'll bathe them."

He rose and then sat down, as she had told him. And then she saw a curious thing. She stared at it appalled, half-kneeling in front of him. He said, "What is it?"

"Your hair."

"My what?"

Of course he didn't know. She hesitated, beginning to lave his feet. He put up his hand to his head. "Seems all right."

"It's turned gray," said Clair gently.

"What!"

Clair kept her head down-bent. Had he been through as bad a time as that? Hers had been nothing to it. Of course he had thought her lost for ever.... His feet made her shudder, and he shuddered himself as she drew out long slivers of stone from one.

"That was from the time I had a slip and glissade on those infernal red hills."

"If only we had something to bind up the cuts with—"

"I'll make sandals from part of this bearskin. That'll do, thanks. Let's get back to the fire."

At the fire Clair knelt and toasted herself some more of the mammoth meat. Sinclair made his moccasins.

"How did you find me?" Clair asked him.

"God knows. How did you get lost?"

SHE told him of the circumstances the while the day brightened; then heard of his own Odyssey. Her absence had not been discovered by him until the afternoon of the day on which she had been lost. He had hunted from group to group, asking about her and finding her nowhere.

Presently the whole camp was aroused and, excepting those Cro-Magnard engaged in the buccaning of the mammoth-meat, every hunter and woman had set out in the search for her.

From one of the hunters the American heard of Clair's joining the party which had made a dash through the hills to intercept the second mammoth. Thereat, in company with Aerte and three or four more, he had set out to retraverse that route. In a muddy patch on the other side of these hills, he had come on the imprint of a recent footstep which he knew was Clair's.

"How did you know?"

From the arching of the instep. There had been no more than that single footprint, but it had pointed southward, toward a range of hills. He had set out to reach that range.

The range had been gained as the darkness was falling, and with no further sign of Clair, nor sound of her or answer to his shouts. He had hunted the range all the night, and with the coming of morning had gained the top of it and considered the situation, deciding correctly that if Clair lost were still Clair alive she must have determined to make the southward mountains in the hope of intercepting the trek of the Cro-Magnards. So he himself had set out in the direction of the nameless Alps and—then he had heard her hail him.

She said: "We've always been cut apart and strangers in some way, Keith. Why did you do it?—all this tremendous search for me?"

He had made the moccasins by then and was fitting them to his feet with gut as string. He looked across the savanna to the mountains.

"Any of the hunters would have done it. Aerte is probably searching for you still."

"Yes, I know. But we are different. So why?"

He said in a very still, strained voice: "It's because I love you, I suppose. And there isn't any supposing about it. It's just that."

She stared into the fire. "And I love you also. I think I always loved you. From that day I saw you on the gallery of the *Magellan*. Remember it—twenty-five thousand years ago? Oh, Keith!"

He dropped the moccasins and came toward her, gray-haired, his eyes alight. She shook her head. She spoke in a whisper. "But there's still Aerte—my husband for the dark days."

"Eh?"

"He's as remote and impossible as a boy in a fairy tale. But I'm his and he's mine for the dark days at least. I thought you were Aerte last night. I could have sworn you were."

He sat down again. He said, "It's damned nonsense."

"I know."

"Aerte will make no claim on you if you come to me."

"No, he won't. But that's the point, Keith. Oh, my dear, don't you see? It's for you and your sake and the sake of your dream that I must keep by Aerte. Unless you've given that up? Are we to look for the hunters again?"

He nodded south toward the mountains. His face had the savage sulkiness of repressed wrath she remembered from the days of crossing the upland plateau. "We'll go on and wait their coming there. Even if they don't go farther than this stretch of country we'll be able to see them and return to them."

"But you want them to go farther? You're going to lead them south of the mountains and find a river and plant corn and teach them to build houses and cast metals? Remember? You and I are going to change the course of history there, somewhere beyond these Alps. Do you think we can do it without keeping faith in every detail with the hunters? They'd laugh and say nothing and only pity Aerte a little, but they'd never take counsel from you again."

Sinclair sat down and completed the binding of his footwear. Clair laughed, a little shakily.

"It's me or the future of history, Keith! . . . And don't leave it to me now, else I'll forget that other lover of mine who died on the wire in France, and I'll forget all the black oppressions done in this wild world under the sun, and think only of you."

He said: "I think you've cured me. Bless you. We'll go south and await the coming of Aerte and the hunters."

"OH, that light last night. I forgot to mention it."

"Eh?"

They were on the road to the southern mountains, though no road had ever crossed that wild belt of land. It was past noon. Here and there the snow still lay in patches, or shivered and wilted into slush pools under the heat of the sun. And over all the landscape was a steaming haze that rose a little, but patched the ground in great areas to indistinctness.

They had crossed a good eight or nine miles of country since leaving the encampment of the night before. Now the mountains before them changed shape continually, but visibly grew greater. Crowned with snow, the great massif stretched from horizon to horizon, with in front, left-ward, an extended arm, a jumble of broken peaklets and poised glacierettes. Somewhere in that extended arm, Clair thought, she had seen the light.

Sinclair scowled down at her questioningly. "Light? What kind?"

She put her arm through his. "Funny how that scowl of yours used almost to intimidate me! . . . Fun to be alive, isn't it, Keith?"

The scowl went from his face. He pinched her shoulder absently. Then: "The light?"

"Oh, yes. It was like a camp-fire."

"Couldn't be. At least, I don't think so. The hunters have no story of other groups living so comparatively near."

Some half-memory vexed her mind. "But there might be."

"I don't know." They passed into a winding trackway made by beasts, between two stretches of marsh, and climbed up from that low patch to firmer ground. "There might be, but on the whole I doubt it. Our hunters are perhaps as yet the only human beings in Atlantis—perhaps in all the world."

She found that a breath-taking notion. "But there were other peoples in pre-history besides the Cro-Magnards."

"Later, yes. But at this epoch? Mayn't the others have been helped into full humanity by imitation of our proto-Cro-Magnards? . . . We can't say. But all these things are accidental, dependent on a multitude of chances that might arise in one district and nowhere else. Perhaps in the world at the moment there are only tribes of submen at various levels, and our hunters constitute the only group that has as yet emerged into full humanity."

"Then—"

He smiled down into her grave face, Clair looked back at the land behind them.

"Any accident changes the nature of things forever. If our Cro-Magnards were suddenly wiped out—"

"There might never be such a thing as history. At least—we can never know."

"Oh, the awful loneliness of men! They couldn't help making gods
when they found some shelter and security in an agricultural society.
. . . Pious rotten romanticism, Keith—remember what you once told
me I was addicted to?—but that night I was lost on the hills back there
I began to think that perhaps there was some God after all. Not just
a god. Something, Some One. . . ."

She looked up at him. Thousands and thousands were yet to look
up into the faces of their fellows for confirmation of that wild hope. . . .
He said: "An honest god's the noblest work of man. I don't believe
there's anything to shield us from the darkness, Clair. And not even for
the sake of poetry should we carry the idea to our hunters in that world
we're to make beyond the mountains. . . . If we ever get beyond them."

"Tremendous things, aren't they?"

They were. Somewhere at the foot of their slopes, however, the Cro-
Magnards would arrive in time, and there was nothing for the two of
them but to press on and await that arrival.

Clair said, being dragged out of a squelchy, boggy place: "The light—
we never settled about that."

"No." Sinclair, assisting her to her feet, abruptly pulled her down
again and lay prone himself. "But we can now, I think."

Clair, her breath shaken from her, wriggled out of his grasp and
looked in the direction in which he pointed.

The tapering tip of the northward spur of the mountain range was
not more than three miles away. The forests climbed its base in green
attack, even skirmished remotely up into valleys and ledges of the
heights. Directly south was the more gigantic background of the range
proper, a good six miles away.

Here and there, in the angle so formed, grew clumps of larch and fir
and great stretches of gorse. Amid these fed the herds of aurochs Clair
had noted before. One herd was very close—a herd that had ceased to
feed and stood on the qui vive, bulls with gigantic tails uplifted, cows
and calves sniffing the air. And the reason for the alarm—a dozen of
reasons—became at length obtrusive to Clair's gaze.

They were less than a quarter of a mile away, but had remained
unperceived by her because of their dull gray coloring. It seemed to
her that it was on all fours they were creeping from bush to bush,
nearer their quarry, the aurochs. But indeed it was merely that their
arms were so elongated as naturally to reach the ground. Across cavern-
ous, hair-matted torsos were strapped crude skin-wrappings. From each
pair of shoulders, on a short squat neck, a strange deformed head, chin-
less, browless, enormously eye-ridged, projected forward so that the

Thing could never look directly upward. Even at that distance they were horrible, dreadful and awful caricatures of familiar lovely things.

"Neanderthalers," said Sinclair.

CHAPTER THIRTEEN—*All Our Yesterdays*

NO SNOW fell that night, but a bitter wind sprang up with the coming of darkness and blew into the great triangular space formed by the forest lines and the bastions of the unknown mountain ranges. At first the darkness,'for there came neither moon- nor star-rise, was heavy and complete, without even the usual brooding Atlantean grayness. And then, as if lighted one by one, there became obvious far in the base of the triangle and ranging up northward toward the open country the glare of great fires.

Sinclair and Clair saw them pringling brightly in the night, from their own camping-place in the heart of a thicket of broom-plants and larch. They also had kindled a fire; they had kindled it midway the thicket, so that there was little chance of those alien fire-tenders seeing it. But both, after they had eaten, went out to the verge of thicket to watch that bright sentineling of the mountain-base. Sinclair stood with his arm round Clair, to still her shivering.

"Then they can make fires—they are men," she said.

"They are men, but not Man. They are the sub-human species that are almost men, and are to be in occupation of most of Europe when our Cro-Magnards wander there thousands of years hence. If they do so wander."

The fires burned steadily. Clair remembered the creeping beasts of the afternoon and shuddered with disgust. Yet perhaps that was unreasonable enough. Perhaps there was nothing of savagery about them, any more than among the Cro-Magnards.

She saw the dim shake of Sinclair's gray head.

"Their conduct didn't warrant it. Men—the Cro-Magnards and the stock that produced ourselves—are decent, kindly animals of anthropoid blood, like the chimpanzee and gibbon. But there is another strain— the gorilla and perhaps these Neanderthalers—the sullen individualist beast whose ferocity is perhaps maladjustment of body and an odd black resentment against life."

His voice sounded absent. "I wonder. . . . Look here, go back to the fire. I'm going out to see what they're really like."

"What?" She was startled enough at that. "Then I'll come as well."

"Can't. One of us must go, Clair, and must take the bearskin for

covering against this infernal wind. And it must be me. I'm stronger
than you are and I can run faster."

"But why must? We needn't go near them at all."

"We must because our hunters will be down from the north in the
next day or so, and there's no telling what will happen then. If they're
peaceable or cowardly beasts there's nothing to fear. If not—"

"But we needn't lead the Cro-Magnards anywhere near them. We can
take them through the mountains away over there, somewhere." She
pointed to the right in the westward darkness.

"Can we? I wonder. . . . I must go, Clair."

She said, standing beside the fire and helping him to tie the bearskin:
"Do take care of yourself, my dear." And thought, "As though we were
in Kensington and I was telling him to mind the buses."

He said, absently still, "I'll do that." Then he picked up his spear,
and put his hand on her shoulder and gave it a little shake, and went
off into the darkness.

Clair built up the fire and lay down in the shelter of the break-wind.
She took her own spear beside her for company and Sinclair's bow as
well, though she knew nothing of the handling of the thing. It was a
very lonely vigil. The fire fluffed and rose and fell occasionally in eddies
of the wind. But presently that wind died away almost completely,
though the cold seemed to grow intenser still.

Where were Aerte and the hunters?

Something bayed close at hand beyond the bushes. There came a
distant scuffling; nearer, the swift scurry of running paws. The scurry
ceased. Then a pad-pad-padding began in a circle, just beyond the range
of the fire-glow. Clair, with a very dry throat, stirred the fire and in
its increase of radiance saw that she was surrounded by a pack of
wolves—beasts with long feathery brushes and brightly erected ears.

Each might have been of the bigness of an Alsatian. Sometimes they
sat and rested, staring at her, at other times resumed that scurrying en-
circlement of the fire. It was difficult to realize that if they overcame fear
of the fire they could eat her, sink those bright teeth into her legs and
throat and stomach, in a flounder of hot and stench-laden bodies. . . .

Clair got to her feet once and waved her spear at a great cadaverous
brute. He stopped in his pacing, head brightly alert, and cocked his ears.
Then, as though grinning sardonically, he bared his teeth, growled and
advanced a step or so. Clair stirred the fire again, and he retreated.

So the night went on. Clair, sitting dozing once, awoke to find—not the
beasts upon her as she had dreamed—and dreaming had awoke with a
startled cry—but them gone and the fire burned very low, and herself

very cold. She fed the smolder hurriedly, carefully. A mammoth trumpeted, southward, the sound eery and plaintive.

The clouds began to clear and presently, with a faint spraying of powdery light, the star-rise came. Clair sat and warmed herself and got up and walked about and sat down again. Still Sinclair did not return.

There came a breath of dawn through the air of the darkness. The stars grew brighter and then faded. And through the dawn Sinclair came back. She heard him calling in the distance, "Clair! Clair!" and ran and found him.

He had been *lost.*

"MOST infernally lost." He was splashed with mud and rimed with frost. His eyebrows and eyelids curled white with frost. He sat down jerkily by the fire and started up again, glancing over his shoulder. "Idiotic to shout, but there was nothing else to be done. I hadn't a notion of where you were. Lost my way completely coming back—as I might have guessed I'd do. . . . Wonder if they heard me shouting?"

"I'll go and see," Clair said.

He pulled her down beside him. "Not that, anyway," he said grimly.

They listened to that austere world of the Third Interglacial awakening with the coming of the morning over the Atlantean savanna. Sparrows chirped in the trees. Somewhere in the depths of the wood a corn-crake was sounding its note. Spite the nearing of the sun, it was still bitterly cold. But there was no crackling of the undergrowth under coming feet.

"What are they like?" Clair whispered.

"God. . . . Awful."

He said no more than that about them. Instead, he shivered. Clair cut meat from their dwindling supply and grilled it. Sinclair was nodding from lack of sleep. She asked: "Did you get near them?"

"I lay above one of their caves. I seemed to lie there for hours. Limestone spur, that, and its upper tip here is honeycombed with caves. There must be several hundreds of them. Ugh!"

She ruffled his gray hair. "Don't think of them or speak about them for a bit. Do you think I could use your bow?"

"Why?"

She looked wistfully through the trees toward the sound of the forest fowls. "I would like chicken for a change."

He smiled at her from a face as gray as his hair. "Try. But don't go too far. And if you see—any of them—scream like hell and run back in this direction." . .

She went through the morning-stirred forest, thinking, at first almost
in a panic, "I had to get away. . . . Keith, my dear, you've had the
devil of a night. Will it pass or are you ill? . . . Oh, *damn* this thing."

She stopped and disentangled the bow from a bush, and hurried on
again because of the coldness. She came to the edge of a clearing. In the
charred forest-litter two birds fed, perkily, with quick-darting heads.
Partridges. She thought: "I'll never hit them," and stopped, and planted
the butt of the bow in the ground, and fitted the clumsy arrow. One
of the birds saw her and raised its head, regarding her sidewise, out of
a bright questioning eye. Her fingers fumbled frozenly at the bow-string.
Now.

The arrow whizzed across the space, an enormous lance of a
projectile. One partridge rose with a flirr! The other lay impaled wing
from wing, and fluttering wildly. Clair wrung its neck and tried to get
out the arrow, and desisted, lest she snap off the insecure flint; and went
back toward Sinclair and the camp-fire. The break-wind shelter was
deserted. She dropped the bird and ran through the trees toward the
open country that led to the Neanderthal caves.

Sinclair turned about as he heard her coming.

"Sh! For God's sake!"

The great triangle was evidently the hunting ground of the beast-men.
Three separate parties, none of them near enough for the intimate study
of individuals, were debouching in various directions from that far
mountain-wall—one party apparently heading in the direction of their
shelter. A little over two miles away, Clair judged it. Sinclair swore,
ruffling his bearded chin.

"Are they on my track—or is it just a chance drift after game?"

Clair stared with him. He gave a sigh of relief. "A chance party, after
all. They're just on the prowl."

"Are they? They're not coming in a straight line, but they seem to
be following something. Didn't you lose yourself last night? Perhaps
they're following your—"

"By God, they are!"

A LL that forenoon they fled westward and southwestward, the gray
beasts behind them. Sinclair's own running abilities might have out-
distanced them with ease, but Clair needed frequent rest. Once or
twice, reaching the foot of one or other of the rolling inclines in which
the land ebbed and flowed, they would glance up and see their pursuers
at the summit, sometimes less than a quarter of a mile distant. On flat
country that distance grew greater: the Neanderthalers were at a

disadvantage on the plain. Once when a good mile and a half separated them, Clair, lying panting on the ground, asked:

"Shouldn't we strike north? We'd meet Aerte and the hunters."

Sinclair himself lay and breathed in great gasps, watching that loping, crouched-forward trot of the beast-men. "We might miss them completely. Perhaps they're already much nearer the mountains than we've supposed. Anyhow, they'll descend farther to the west than this, I think. . . . Rested?"

"Goodness, no." She looked at him, white-faced, and smiled. "If only I'd had training as a charwoman instead of as a novelist!"

"You don't do badly." He stood up. A long guttural wail came down the air from the beast-men. "I think they don't like us."

. . . But they followed on behind, doggedly enough, the horrors. Clair, running stripped and unshod, carried nothing but the light spear she had brought from the far northern camp of the Cro-Magnards.

Sinclair had tied to his back both the bearskin, now enwrapping the slain partridge, and his bow and arrows. His feet were still in their moccasins, and from the bloody tracks left behind by his companion he could see that without such aids Clair herself was hardly capable of keeping the pace for long.

Open country they had come to then. But the Neanderthalers seemed tireless. Sinclair looked back to see them not more than half a mile away. Did they recognize Clair and himself as kindred animals, to be killed as freaks, or did they seem just desirable and tirable meat?

Messy end, too. For Clair—? Not to be thought of.

But it had to be thought of. He said: "If they overtake us. Clair, I'll kill you. That'll be best. It won't hurt much."

"Oh, don't be a fool!"

He almost sulked, and grinned wryly at the recurrence of his ancient short-temper. Clair flung herself to the ground again.

"Can't go farther—yet. Sorry I said that, Keith. But you are a fool to suggest these melodramatics, you know. . . . Here, in Atlantis. Stuff out of Victorian novels. . . . And I ought to suggest now that you should leave me and save yourself. Not so silly. Oh, goodness, my heart! . . . We'll just fight it out together. They'll kill both of us."

"Will they?" He stood above her, desperate, looking backward.

"Of course they will. Oh, because I'm a woman? I'll seem just as repulsive to them as they do to us. . . . How far?"

"Very near now."

He had unslung his bow. Clair scrambled to her knees. The beast-men were quite close, running with lowered heads and trailing fringes of body-hair, their knuckles touching the ground at every forward swing of their bodies, in their hands great shapeless mallets of stone, mounted on rude wooden hafts. Sinclair knelt on one knee. The bow-string sang like a plucked guitar.

A Neanderthaler to the left—not one Sinclair had aimed at—received the arrow in his chest, almost in the region of the heart. The brute screamed horribly, and its companions, swaying and lurching, halted.

The beast plucked stupidly at the arrow, and then bent its head and bit the thing clean off where the shaft entered its chest. Then it suddenly crumpled, as though some support had been withdrawn. Sinclair loosed his second arrow, glanced after it not at all, but heard its thud in flesh and the succeeding howl; and dragged Clair to her feet.

"Try again."

They ran hand in hand toward the near belt of forest.

Clair felt her lungs bursting. A red mist played before her eyes. Twice she tripped, and Sinclair, savagely, jerked her to her feet again. Again and again the earth seemed to rise up toward her. Sinclair's grasp on her hand suddenly eased. She heard his voice far off.

"Done all we can. Sit down, my dear."

She fell rather than sat, and put her hands to throbbing ear-drums. Sinclair gave a shout.

"Impossible! . . . They've turned!"

Clair swung round at that, resting on her elbows also, looking. The Neanderthalers were in retreat, carrying the dead body. One of them went with limp-swinging arm, blood-dripping. Every now and then he bent to bite at the arm. Clair stared stupidly.

"They're going."

He lay beside her, almost exhausted as she was. "Looks like it."

THEY had neither the will nor the breath to say more at the moment. Meantime the Neanderthalers, without a backward glance, shambled across the savanna, topped a low rise and disappeared into the jungle wilderness in the direction of the northern spur. It was past noon. Still there was no sunlight and still it blew as harshly as during the night. Sinclair, with a driving headache, sat erect.

"Can't stay here. Die of cold after the heat of that run. I'll leave you the bearskin and go and make a fire over there."

Clair sat up also. She had the pocked gray face of a woman of fifty. "I'll come. I can manage."

Somehow they helped each other to the forest-fringe—great beeches standing with shrill whistling boughs. But farther in were more larch, and then a wide grove of stone-oaks. Beyond these: more evergreens, then a wide glade and open country once more.

Through the glade the open country to the west showed up as differing in no great degree from the stretches they had already traversed. They dropped to earth by a little stream meandering amid the tree-roots—an indifferent little stream crooning in an absorbed contentment—and drank ice-cold water which instantly gave Clair cramp. Sinclair picked her up and carried her under a larch near by.

"Stick it. I'll have a fire in a minute."

It seemed to Clair an unending minute. Then she was conscious of warmth and of Sinclair kneeling, massaging her. He had the fire kindled and crackling. The grayness had gone from his face, and from her own.

"Feel better?"

"Leagues. Goodness"—she looked up at him in the gay, ironic self-appraisal that survived the *Magellan*, clothes, comfort and seemingly every conceivable contingency—"*and* hungry!"

"I know. So'm I. Nothing like a run in the Neanderthal Stakes for an appetite. I'm roasting your partridge."

It smelled savory enough. Clair sat up and assisted. They sat side by side, and despite her hunger and her recovery she still felt weak, and leaned her head comfortably on Sinclair's shoulder.

She dozed a little. So did Sinclair. Then their heads knocked together and they started awake. The smell of singeing partridge filled the air. Clair shook herself.

"Shockingly selfish again. It's you who've a right to be sleepy. Rest when we've had lunch."

"I will. I'm almost all in."

They ate nearly all the partridge. It was very good. Sinclair, lying down and closing his eyes, nevertheless did so with a mental reservation. He would keep awake and get up in a short time and make her take his place. . . . He looked at her from below half-closed eyelids that each seemed to weigh a ton. God, if the Neanderthalers. . . .

Infernal to die and never see Clair again, never hear her deep, enjoyable and enjoying laughter; or see that bright naive puzzling glance of hers. Infernal to have died and never held her in your arms and kissed her, as she deserves to be kissed.

Never see the Cro-Magnards again, perhaps. We'll go west, far off, and find a passage through the south mountains together, and build a house next spring. Together ourselves. Together. . . .

Clair's voice raised in excitement, her hand shaking him. "Keith—oh, Keith, our hunters!"

HE HAD slept for perhaps a couple of hours, in spite of his resolution. He sat up with a start and looked round scowlingly. "The hunters?"

"I'm sure they are. Away over there by that cramped little wood."

He saw them then. "The hunters right enough." His voice was oddly unglad. "Still on the trek, too."

They had debouched from the wood that Clair thought of as cramped. They were specks in distance, but speck-men, not the strange beasts of Neanderthal. They straggled southward in happy-go-lucky migration, moving slowly, proving they had no lack of food at least at the moment.

Sinclair got to his feet stiffly.

"No more Neanderthalers, anyhow. And you'll find Aerte again."

"I needn't. We need never find any of them."

He started: "You've thought that?"

"And you?"

He nodded. Clair said slowly:

"We could hide from them and wait till they pass. We could go south beyond the mountains, and start a Golden Age of our own. We could be happier than was ever possible in the world—before or after. . . . And we'd be ashamed of ourselves all our lives."

He found a wry gibe: " 'Stern daughter of the voice of God!' "

She laughed pitifully, looking out at the nearing Cro-Magnards. Was ever such a fantastic choice before a man and woman? Sinclair wondered. And wondering, he knew there was no choice, neither for himself nor for Clair.

For she brought out of that dim twentieth century of three weeks ago the memory of her boy fiancé who had screamed away a night of agony beyond the parapets of Mametz; and he—he had brought memories kin enough to hers, dying soldiers and starving miners, the Morlocks of the pits. . . . Clair seemed to have read his thoughts.

"We're both playing, Keith, and we know it. Let's go out to them." She turned away, and then turned back. "But you'd like to kiss me first!"

When he had finished with that they went out across the cold knee-length grass, laden as they had arrived. The whole migration of the hunters paused, in straggling, shimmering lines in the cold gold light of the afternoon. And then there came a shout.

They had been recognized.

Clair had been lost and she was found. She felt no repulsion toward Aerte. Only pity. Sinclair had gone back to his place by the fire of Aitz-kore. Life went on—life in a dream in winter-threatened Atlantis.

CHAPTER FOURTEEN—*Now Sleeps the Crimson Petal*

A ND THE unaccustomed cold grew ever more intense. Day came and
brought no lightening of that burden. Instead, it brought generally
sharp showers of hail in the morning hours and at noon the scurry of a
snow-blizzard from the northwest. It was weather of a severity the
hunters had never known before.

Stumbling campward at evening both hunters and Sinclair's scouts
would come on the bodies of their fellows lying frozen and naked in
places where exhaustion had overtaken them. Winter had come to
Atlantis—a foretaste of that winter that was gradually creeping down on
all the northern hemisphere, presently to crystallize into the spreading
glaciers and the long silences of the Fourth Ice Age.

Game grew ever scarcer. The herds went west and disappeared, and
the hunters might have trailed in pursuit but for the alien presence of
Sinclair in their midst. Hence the scouts that day after day went out
under his direction, puzzled yet friendly, even though they might never
return from such scoutings, any more than those death-frozen comrades
of theirs. Game had almost vanished, but packs of the raiding and
scavenging carnivora hung around the camp, and at night the fires had
to be built to twice the usual height, both in order to scare the wolves
and hyaenodon and to counteract the bitter frosts.

On the second day Sinclair himself vanished in early dawn together
with two of the strongest and wiriest Cro-Magnards. It did not snow all
that day, but to Clair, it seemed that the cold had again increased. They
could not long remain in this place.

Indeed, Aerte had told her that they were to follow the game west-
ward on the morrow. He had no understanding of Sinclair's hesitations.
. . . Doubtlessly, however, like other hesitants on other occasions, the
White Hunter would follow the main drift of opinion and migration.

Thus, Aerte, the while Clair marveled, chilledly and once again, at
these people of the dawn. There was no compulsion, just as there was
no acceptance of it. They had grown to know and love Sinclair, perhaps
because of that energetic righteousness of his that was so in contrast
to their own unhesitating and unswerving kindliness. But he was no
magic leader from the void, no story-book hero.

He was merely one who promised good hunting-grounds and pleasant
days beyond the southward mountains. Now it was evident that he was
mistaken, as a man might be. West or east they must go. The game
seemed to have gone west. They would follow it.

That night Sinclair came back with one of his hunters. The other had
been lost in a canyon of the southern mountains, the great black-blue
wall that dominated the horizons of their world. The American came to
Clair while there was still daylight and flung himself down by the fire
deserted but for herself.

He was spattered in mud from head to foot, mud that had frozen on
him; his arms and legs were scored with long cicatrices. For a little he
lay in silence near Clair. She put her hand on his shoulder in that caress
that was his own, and he put up his hand to her hand. He said:

"There's no road at all through the southward mountains. It is an
absolutely impassable wall. We've climbed and prospected ever since we
reached it an hour after daybreak. And the other parties that have gone
into the west report the same. It's a range that may lie midway across
Atlantis. And it curves northward after a bit."

"North?" Clair lay on an elbow and reflected; and suddenly understood. "Then if the hunters go west that will take them into a worse
winter. It might even mean—"

"Extinction. These people can not stick things worse than they are
at present. And it'll grow worse every hour."

"Then what are we going to do?"

"I don't know. God, how I ache!"

He lay so quiet that she thought he was asleep. But presently he spoke
again. "And in the east, beyond that northward-making spur, we know
there are leagues and leagues of brackish marsh. That would mean, if we
turn the drift east, that we'll have to go far north again to circumvent the
marsh, and turn south again. It would mean that hardly a woman or
child could survive. Perhaps not any of us. . . . Remember my Utopia
beyond the mountains?" He laughed.

Clair sat and stared at him and the fading of the daylight. And then a
great light seemed to flash on her:

"But they didn't die, Keith. They went east, somehow, some of them,
and escaped this winter. We know it from history, as you've often told
me. Our hunters weren't killed. They reached France thousands of
years after this."

H E WAS silent for a little, then he said: "That was in the history we
know, not in the history we hope to build."

She put out her hand and shook him again. "Oh, we're playing again,
Keith. *How if the history we know is the history we helped to build?*
How if when you, twenty-five thousand years away, learned as a student
that the Cro-Magnards came into Spain at the end of the Ice Age—

how if you were learning about an event which you yourself had helped to fashion?"

"Then I've come back again and can refuse its fashioning this second chance—even if I knew how." He sat up. "And there is perhaps a way!"

"Which?"

He pondered, looking at her and not seeing her. "The northward spur to the east is broken off from the main mountain-wall. I saw that on the night I crept out from our camp and went to spy on the Neanderthalers. There's a long hillocky valley lies between. Perhaps half a mile broad.

"Keith, you've found the way!"

"By God, I have not! Oh, we're the stuff of dreams, but that's not the dream I'm going to help humanity to dream. We'd crawl through that pass some time at night, so's not to arouse the Neanderthalers, and gain the country in the east. I don't know how many would ever gain it, but some at least. Not me among them, I think. And beyond that pass in the east lies: Your boy fiancé dying on the wire in France, Clair, and the crucified slaves along the Appian Way and the Pinkertons shooting down the starving strikers of a Scotch philanthropist. . . . Not if I know it! Better to end it here. Better to make this the end of the human adventures."

"Here's your hunter, Clair. Twenty-five thousand years hence he'll also be a hunter—of human heads in New Guinea, with dried human hands strapped on his chest. Or a gangster in Chicago. Or a Steel Helmet in Germany. Like it?"

Aerte sat down beside them. He looked from one to the other with puzzled eyes.

She could find no words that did not seem trite and pitiable ones.

"There were other people than the head-hunter and the gangster. . . . There was Karl Liebknecht; there was Anatole France. There was even yourself in that age of which we came. There was I."

He turned back at that. She saw more than a bitter denial in his face now. She looked at Aerte and some one other than herself spoke through her lips:

"Do you think they ever quite beat us, Keith—the beasts of civilization? Do you think that Aerte ever quite died, away there in those years? Do you think he won't beat them when civilization has passed and finished? Remember Sir John?—The hunter will come again in the world we left! You and I and thousands of others were fighting up from the fears and cruelties of civilization to look at the world through his eyes again.

"There are later ages than the one we came from, and Aerte—he'll

walk across the world again, and fearless, but with Orion's sword in
his belt and the Milky Way for a plaything. The moaning and the tears
—they're a darkness yet to fall on our hunters. But it will pass. I know.
You know it will. And it is for that though your own dream of changing
that chance must finish, that you are to lead the Cro-Magnards east to
the pass in the mountain-wall."

She could not see when she stopped speaking. She thought: "Oh! I
ache also, and I'm cold and hungry, and I've been ranting. . . . And
I'd like to lie down and sleep and sleep and forget it all—" She heard
Sinclair speaking, and looked up and saw that Titan resentment gone
from his face.

"You've won again, Clair. There was you, at least, in that age that is
not yet. . . . We'll go east tomorrow."

A T DAWN the next morning the Cro-Magnards moved out from their
camp and stood up the line of march to the east. In front Sinclair
and his surviving scout vanished beforehand. Clair marched midway
the migration in the company of a girl, Lizair, who had adopted her
after the death of Zumarr; it was the same girl who had refused her
first suitor in the time of the mating for the dark days.

Now the boy whom she had chosen walked beside them. Aerte had
gone off with a band of other hunters to forage northward for game.

No sun came, but a pale diffusion of saffron light in the east. The
wind had died away again, but beyond the forest belt to the verge of
which the Neanderthalers had pursued Clair and Sinclair, the Cro-
Magnards saw the rolling savanna pelted with flying showers of sleet.

Here, also, the snow lay deeper than in the higher country from which
they had descended, and the trek, a gray trek in a gray country, moved
slowly enough in the direction set by Sinclair the night before. Children
wailed ceaselessly in the piercing chill. Behind, as Clair could see looking
back, there followed pack on pack of wolves.

Clair tramped half that day like one in a dream. And in a dream she
saw the country close in and open out before them; she was hazily conscious of the passing bombardments of sleet; once of a thunderstorm
and a great flare of lightning that played over a wood where they halted
somewhere toward midday and ate cooked or raw flesh brought with
them, for Sinclair had told them to light no fires.

It was there that the girl Lizair began to cough and cough in ever-
increasing spasms, until she was coughing blood, and in a little while
was dead. They left her there, and others, and the wolves halted for a
little time, and then came on again.

The northward spur, not more than five miles or so away, was reddened with the colors of the sunset when Sinclair and his scout fell back on the main body of the trek. Clair was told of their coming and managed to urge her half-frozen limbs to carry her to the front of the march. As she did so the march gradually turned aside, to the south, making another small wood. Sinclair had advised a halt.

She found him at last, Aitz-kore and a group of other Cro-Magnards about him. They were at the farther verge of the wood in which the trek had halted, and in the hearing of the long, easy agglutinative role of the proto-Basque speech she stood for a while puzzled and unnoticed. Then she heard her name mentioned, and saw Sinclair's face lighten. She went forward and touched his arm then.

He held her in his arms then, while the hunters with troubled eyes looked at them. "How are you?"

She was weak enough to want to sob, but she did not. "I'm lasting, but there have been awful things back there, Keith."

"I've heard. It can't be helped. We must just go on."

"Can we?"

He indicated the open country in front of them. It was the triangle of the Neanderthalers, and apparently quite deserted. "That other chap and I have been watching the place ever since we arrived early this forenoon. There's been no one out on it, and no sign of any of the beastmen stirring, even over by the spur."

Clair peered through the intervening distances. She saw, after a little, lighter patches in the face of the cliff, and in that clear, generally untainted air, there was the ghost of a sharp, blue odor.

"Aren't those their fires?"

"Yes. But they don't seem to be moving out of the caves. Probably they have plenty of food and will continue to keep inside as they have done all through the daylight. We'll strike south as soon as the darkness comes and wait on the lee of the mountain-wall for the stars—if there are any. Can't move farther in pitch blackness. Then we'll cross and push up through the valley."

"If there's fighting—what will happen?"

"God knows. Our hunters have never fought anything but beasts. They can't conceive a human enemy. It would all depend if they were to find the Neanderthalers human or bestial. . . . We won't have any need to put it to the test, I think. . . . Go and help every one on the move or interested, Clair. No fires. . . . Eh?"

She gave a little ghost of a laugh. " 'While shepherds watched their flocks by night'—I never thought I'd play the role. I wish we could sing."

"What would you sing?"

"Something comforting."

"Do, then; but not too loud. It'll keep the hunters interested."

She had never thought of singing to them before. They had no songs of the European type, with sharp rhymes and mechanical spacings. But they came round about, from the grayness of the trees, in some numbers as she began to sing, her voice a little hoarse, for she shivered still, but as sweet and sensuous as it had ever been.

> "Abide with me,"
> "Fast falls the eventide,
> The darkness deepens,
> Lord, with me abide."

THE wind rose again. The last of the daylight lingered sharply, on pinpoints of the strange world in the beginning of history, and Sinclair's eyes, in a sudden passion of knowledge of how little of this world he had ever made deep acquaintance with, went from point to point as these rear-guards of the day quenched their lamps and departed.

He looked up at the sky. It was pall-black. He moved and stamped frozen feet, thinking: "I'll have frost-bite soon. And Clair—better not think of her. Of nothing but the pass. God, if only there will be starshine!"

He waited while he counted a thousand, and then moved through the darkness of the trees, speaking to the hunters and women. They must walk four or five abreast and follow after him. He heard their pleasant singsong of response, though many of their faces he could not see, and turned about, and called that he was ready, and held out gingerly southward on the track he had mentally plotted while the daylight lasted. He held his spear extended, and groped the path with it.

He thought, "Rotten show if the wolves attack."

Beyond the wood the wind smote them as with keen-edged knives. Sinclair gasped, and steadied himself, and plodded forward. Behind, he heard the scuffle of the migration, and looking over his shoulder could see the lighter shadows that were the bodies of the frontward Cro-Magnards. One slipped forward to his side and kept pace with him. Sinclair said: "Who are you?"

"I am Aerte."

"You had better go back to Clair and guard her. I can lead the way."

Aerte, the Atlantean child-man whom he had never been able to detest, whom even in bitterest moments he had regarded only with gray acquiescence, remained at his shoulder. "Clair sent me here."

So that was that. . . .

Once the wolves behind did verily attack, and the whole column swayed and eddied while the rearward hunters turned about and fought and stabbed at the leaping bodies in the darkness. They did it with little noise, and the beasts drew off again. But they took with them the bodies of some half-dozen, half-grown children. Nothing could be done for these, and some hunters also did not return. The march through the darkness went on. Sinclair ran back to Clair.

'We're going into something twice as bad as we've had to face in the last hour," Sinclair told her.

"We're turning toward the valley, now?"

"Yes. It's grown a little lighter." His fingers touched hers awkwardly. "Good luck!"

She would have called him back; but he had gone. In another moment, slowly, in a light that gradually increased with the coming of the star-rise through the frost, the trek was again in motion. The wind blew not behind them now, but on their left. And suddenly, pricking out the bastions of the northward mountain-spur, there shone bright and splendid the fires of the Neanderthal caves.

A murmur arose from the Cro-Magnards, but died away at the urgings of Sinclair and Aerte. Over there was danger, no food or help. They must still even the crying of the babies.

The fires seemed to Clair to draw nearer in leaps and bounds. They were fires remote in caves; however, there were no signs of watchers. Right ahead, where the column wound into the presumed valley, was unspotted darkness.

Clair became aware of the fires passing on her left. They had entered the valley. They stumbled up over rocky ground. Clair raised her head once and saw the rocky heavens, unclouded, banded with the glory of the Milky Way.

And then presently another line of fires gleamed directly ahead, a strange, wild moaning filled the air, and above it rose shout on shout—shouting in Sinclair's voice!

The migratory column of the Cro-Magnards was being attacked at a dozen points by the Neanderthalers of the unsuspected valley caves.

THAT had been hours ago.

Morning in the air again. It seemed to Clair, looking downward and around, that this was the land of morning. How many of them had she seen come over the strange pale hills? Would she see this one?

They were through now, the bulk of the frightened, amazed, uncom-prehending Cro-Magnards and their women. Or such of them as had survived the attacks. Or such of them as had not been dragged into those caves of night. . . .

Like a pelting rush of shadows. But shadows of sickening substance, with the gleam of low-set eyes in the foreheadless heads. They charged again, with their undulating moan rising to a scream, and the musk odor of their bodies was sickening. Sinclair's yell met the scream, and at sound of it the Cro-Magnards still unpast the valley point bunched forward uncertainly to meet the attack. . . . Sinclair himself Clair saw, dimly, stripped of bearskin cloak and every other encumberment, in his hand a great club of the beast-men.

Then the scurry of furred gray bodies was upon the Cro-Magnard line.

The morning seemed to have heard the impact. It was coming more quickly out of the wild, unknown, eastern lands. Clair felt its pale fore-radiance in her face as she darted here and there, heeding to the onward guiding of the main hunter-stream. Between two rocks they filed, into the valley-country beyond. Clair thought, "Will they never get through?" and heard herself chanting again foolishly, "Oh—do please hurry!"

Sinclair, on the westward slope, heard that cry. Then other interests engaged him. A great brute tore the club from his hands and took him by the throat. Its breath was fetid in his face. He kicked it, viciously, with a moccasined foot. It screamed and slipped away from him.

The Neanderthalers were swaying backward and downward again, moaning as they retreated. But, as throughout the hours since the migration had stumbled upon the fact that all one valley-wall was inhabited, other gray beasts were coming at a scrambling, swaying run to replace the rout. Tireless, scores on scores of them, reenforcements from the northward spur. Rational animals. Men almost. . . .

Lighter and lighter the darkness. It was gloaming. Sinclair heard Clair, far up the slope:

"Keith! Keith! All the women are through!"

He stumbled up through the ring of hunters toward the ring of her voice. Dawn near. White in the ghostly radiance. "Unhurt?"

He breathed sobbingly. "All right. Every one through?"

"Except those dozen with you."

"I'll send them up. Hurry on yourself."

"You're coming?"

"I'll come. In a minute." He grinned at her. "Do please hurry!"

He watched her disappear. He found himself sobbing again. Now the false dawn illumined the valley.

It rose in a cone, midway, and at the cone-tip the cliffs closed in on either side, allowing barely more than the passage of two men abreast. The red sandstone rocks were already a dun-rose color, though no sign of the actual sun came yet. It was snowing fleecily, but even as he turned back toward the westward slopes that ceased. Now in the morning light added to the light of the cave-fires, he saw the valley alive, like a spider's nest, with fresh hordes of the gray-furred beast-men.

They would follow on in hundreds. . . .

"Go through! Go through!"

Panting, leaning against a rock, he saw them file past, the last of the hunters. Below, the gray hirsute whirlpool beginning to boil again. . . . Two or at least one must stay with him; he could not do it alone. But whom? Not that old man. Nor this boy. Quick, quick. Whom? Whom? Aerte to guard Clair in the world beyond—ah, God, she had still her hunter! He heard himself shout with sudden strength:

"Turn south beyond this valley if you can! Keep watch always."

"But you will be there with us, brother." The last hunter, scarred and torn, swayed round and waited. Keith Sinclair cursed him.

"Go on! Go on!"

He heard the pad of retreating feet.

He found himself alone.

He started up, gripping his spear. He peered in the faces of the two who stood beside him.

Clair said, sitting down with a sigh: "Silly to think you could hold this place alone, Keith. So Aerte and I have come back."

The light grew brighter on the hunter's face. Sinclair stared at the two of them. Clair leaned her chin in her hands.

"Nightmare, Keith—but a wonderful one. Last dawn in Atlantis! . . ."

Thereat the sunrise, in a great hush that seemed to hold quiescent even the gathering attack of the Neanderthalers twenty yards below, sped suddenly up from the eastern end of the canyon and poured liquid through the narrow defile.

Clair's head now nodded on her shoulders. But she started up at Sinclair's last cry of entreaty.

"Clair!"

She stumbled between the two men. Her eyes turned to the horror below. "I'll stand behind with my spear. They're coming."

Twice they had come, and twice broken and shambled downward in screaming flight. Clair's spear was gone, the head embedded in a beast-man's chest. Sinclair leaned against the canyon wall, his right arm hanging by a pinch of skin, blood pouring from a dreadful stomach wound. . . . His face a battered mask, all human likeness had gone from the hunter. But she saw his eyes turned toward her, glazing eyes lovely and human still. He staggered to his feet. She felt suddenly serene.

"Oh, my dears, it isn't long now! They are coming again—"

CHAPTER FIFTEEN—*I Shall Arise Again*

SHE awoke in a dazzle of sunshine that blinded her for a moment. She sat up and knuckled her eyes. She felt very tired—sun-tired, as though she had slept a long time in this warmth of the earth and sky. There was a continual drumming splash near at hand, like the sound of the sea heard far off.

She was lying on a patch of sand on a low beach that sloped up to rocky verdant mountains. The violent green of the near underbrush waved, languid and warm, in the ghost of a breeze. Overhead was a sky deep and blue and touched with a sailing speck-net of clouds. A score of yards away the sea rumbled unhurrying on the beach.

"Keith! Aerte!"

A gull whooped past her. Far up the mountainside a sudden roar grew to a grinding clamor, became a glittering snake in the sunlight, hissed; swept from view again. A railway train. . . .

She stared upward in paralyzed affright. Delirium. Of course it was delirium. For suddenly she had remembered. She was dead.

Morning—pass—the Neanderthalers—their last charge—a great malachite club descending—Aerte and Keith gold and white and red-streaked veinings of foam under a wave of snarling grayness. She must still be alive and in delirium—the last alive of the *Magellan*.

She closed her eyes again, that the horror might pass, and willed to die also; and the wind touched her cheek and her hair came ruffling across her face, tickling her skin so that her hand went up involuntarily to put it aside. She opened her eyes on the green warm day. And then she saw something lying a few yards off.

It was Keith Sinclair.

He lay unmoving, face downward in an outpost of the mountain grass. Kneeling in a blur of tears beside him, she thought: "I am mad; it is still delirium." For his body was unmarked by signs of struggle in the pass—She shook his shoulder.

"Keith. Oh, Keith, make it real!"

For answer he yawned where he lay, stretched his arms, stretched his legs, seemed to stretch every muscle in his body. Then, slowly and casually, he turned round and sat erect. He blinked, knuckling his eye as she had knuckled hers. She sat back and watched him.

As she did so there came again, far up the slope, that muffled roar, the green of the mountain vegetation stirred ever so slightly, and again that metal toy monster swept around a curve and vanished with a loud whistle. Sinclair's head jerked upward. He stared with fallen jaw. Then he looked round him, smiled dazedly at Clair.

"By God," he said, *"we're back!"*

Then, "We'll go exploring in a minute. Azores or Madeira I should think. . . . Oh, I'm real enough. . . . Convinced?"

She said, her voice muffled in his long hair: "Oh, my dear! You're real and whole. . . . And ten minutes ago your arm was hanging by a thread from your shoulder—and that stomach-wound—"

Sinclair held her close. "But it wasn't ten minutes ago. It happened thousands of years ago, else we'd never see that train."

His arms about her still, he stared suddenly; laughed.

"What is it?"

"We were killed, of course—and by some chance didn't die. . . . We're back in 1932—unless some other accident has happened. It may be 2000."

She withdrew her head and looked at the brightening day. "Real. You and the world and myself. . . . And I know it's the year we left."

"So do I," he confessed. And thought aloud, "The railway trains of 2000 won't burn coal—"

"Keith, where are we?"

"Eh?" He looked round the scene again. Then: "We're in Morning Pass still. Look."

He pointed to the mountain-edge near at hand. Dimly, a ghostly scene in the sunlight, a remembrance shaped in Clair's mind. That boulder, that curve of rock that swept into the sea where the gray men mustered for their last attack. . . . But the left-ward wall of the pass had vanished into a smother of grass that was presently sand; beyond that also the murmur of the sea. . . . Ten minutes ago, twenty-five thousand years ago. . . . She saw him looking at her in quick understanding.

"We're back, Clair. Don't worry about it. Let's get up and do that exploring."

They stood up together, helping each other. And then it was Sinclair who was seized with an obsessing memory. He looked to right and left and broke away from her, searching. She stared after him.

"Keith!"

He halted in his search, looking over his shoulder. "Aerte—he must be here! He died with us."

But he turned fully round again, and they looked at each other white-faced. And then it seemed to Clair that his face had altered, that she knew at last the meaning of scores of puzzling resemblances that had torn her heart now this way, now that. She said:

"Don't you understand? I do at last. *You are Aerte.*"

THE deserted beach curved northward round the shoulder of the mountain. Out to sea a trail of smoke grew to being across the horizon, became a triune procession of dots that were funnels, and presently sank again. But neither Clair nor Sinclair moved.

"I am Aerte." He sat with his hands clasped round his knees. "Just as he was the boy who died at Mametz and a score of others. Race-type, race-memory, blood of his blood—who can know? . . . And there was a you also in the painted caves. I didn't know them. Now—I saw her a dozen times, in a look, a way of walking. Lizair—she was you."

Clair Stranlay stood with the sun in her face, dreaming also. "Oh, Keith, not only these two! Zumarr and her hunter—Aitz-kore—Lizair's boy-lover who died among the wolves—the young men who came back at evening singing—"

"They're here in the world still, all of them, that company that went over Sun-rise Pass into the morning we never saw."

"But what happened then—that morning? They must have got away."

"Somehow. Perhaps the Neanderthalers never pursued them after our end. Somehow they went east and south and found a place safe from the winter. And then they went east again, into the beginnings of history."

She stood with troubled lighted face, far in dreams, and he looked up at her suddenly with the gaze of the twentieth century.

She smiled into those eyes that were not of the caves of Atlantis.

"Oh, we've awakened. . . ." She looked round the bright weather of the green beach. "We've come back. We'll be hungry in a little, and have to go round the hill, and hear people speak, and wear clothes again, and lie in the little rooms and never hear the midnight cry upon the mountains. That's finished and put by. . . . If only it was a pack of hyaenodon that waited us round that mountain bend!"

It was he who stood up now, with a laugh, and she also saw him with eyes that had lost the acceptance of many a day and scene. Keith Sinclair of the *Magellan*—never that Keith Sinclair again. . . . He smiled down at her. He held out his hand.

"Come along. We'll go and meet the hyaenodon."

She put her fingers in his. "I suppose we must. . . . Love me, my dear?"

"Till the hunters come back to the world again—and after."

She did not stir.

"Then there's still a moment we've never known, Keith, though we dreamed it in the Golden Age. It's still the same sun and earth—for a moment, before we go back to the world that's forgotten both."

Not looking at him, she yet saw his face change strangely, felt the pressure on her fingers alter, knew him kneeling beside her. She put her arms round his neck. He held her away a moment.

"Sure, Clair?"

"Till the hunters walk again."

She drew down his head very slowly, and kissed him tremulously.

SENORA LEIRIA regarded her guest with admiration and uplifted her voice in throaty French.

"But they fit with exactitude!"

The guest raised a flushed smiling face. "Very sweet," she agreed, and thought: "Oh, my good God, and I'll have to wear the things."

The thought was appalling.

Clair sat down. "I'll manage ever so nicely now I've had a bath and you've shown me the stuff I can choose from."

The stout senora lingered, constitutional languor and aroused curiosity in combat. "The dreadful hours you must have spent, Senora Keith, after the wreck of your husband's boat!"

"Shocking." ("If she doesn't go away I'll—")

The door closed. Clair dropped the garments entrusted to her, stumbled to the casement window, and flung it wide open.

"The ghastly, ghastly smell of the place! Just the ordinary room smell? Wonder how Keith's getting on—or what he's getting on? . . . Those must be the roofs of San Miguel over there."

San Miguel of the Azores. . . .

She began to laugh. That servant whom Keith had encountered—

Three hours ago. They'd rounded the mountain bend into view of open cultivated country, a road half a mile away alive with automobiles, and, in the foreground, on a branch of the road, a low and gabled house with a garden and the white shirt-sleeves of a gardener.

Clair had sunk hastily to the ground. "Don't shock them too much, Keith. They've never seen tatters like ours."

He had grinned and set out, long-striding. Almost immediately there was catastrophe. Avoiding the main door and turning rightward through the garden he had collided with a diminutive female in some kind of domestic uniform. Her shrieks preceding him, he had disappeared from Clair's view for a quarter of an hour, and, just as she had begun to

wonder about his safety, had emerged from that main door.
"It's all right, Clair. Put on this coat of the Senora's. We're in the
Azores. Portuguese. I've told them a few lies to avoid explanations."
"Keith—that ulster of yours!" She had struggled into the coat, half-
hysterical. . . . "What were the lies?"
"Coming? Senora Leiria is going to look after you and get you some
clothes. . . . We're the Keiths, an English couple, husband and wife.
Tried to reach San Miguel from Santarem in our three-ton yacht—"
"Are there three-ton yachts?"
"Eh? No idea. But early this morning we met a squall and were upset.
We swam. This is all that's left of our clothes."
"But we'll have to tell some of the truth later."
"We won't be able to avoid that. But this is the best meanwhile.
I've realized just in time that our banks'll refuse us draft, as they'll
believe us lost in the *Magellan*. But I keep an alias account—name of
Keith, League of Militant Pacifist purposes—and can always order on it
by a code message. . . ." They were under the garden wall. "Now—"
Now, with a curious shambling motion, upraised upon the heels of un-
accustomed shoes, Clair Stranlay crossed the floor and began to descend
the stairs. At the foot of the first landing was an open door, and beyond—
"Clair! Hell, what a mess!"
He was tugging to ease an unaccustomed collar.
"Servants! Diseased animals sweating to tend diseased animals! Why
do they? Why the devil do they? Pack a room like this? All this nonsense
of furniture. Pottering in that damned garden. . . . Flowers: they grow
much better wild; any fool knows it. You can see them opposite the
caves—purple-growing blooms."
"Keith!"
She closed the door behind her. He sat down and buried his face in
his hands.
"Sorry. Went crack for a moment. . . . All this—God, we can never
endure it again, Clair! Beyond this house there are the towns and the
filth and the stench. London on a wet Sunday afternoon. The shoddy
crowds of the Boul' Mich'. Newsboys screaming, trains screaming. . . .
It would kill us after—after that."
"What are we going to do, then?"
"Clear out to the South Seas or some such place."
"Escape?"
"Escape."
"My dear, I'd sooner go down to the sea there and walk out into it."
She knelt beside him. "I'm going to do what *you* are going to do. Go

back to the world we came from. Tell them we survived the *Magellan* —and then preach Atlantis to our dying day!"

"Tell them what happened? Who'd ever believe it? Can't you hear the bray of the head-lines?"

She smiled the old gay smile with no irony at all in it. "Different from that. Up-stairs I suddenly knew what we would do. We can't desert the world—we've no right to— Not while there are still Neanderthalers alive—in general's uniforms. Not while they still can lie about the ever-lastingness of rich and poor and innate human ferocity. Not while our hunters are still in the world—somewhere out there, Keith!—chained and gagged and brutalized, begging in streets, cheating in offices, doing dirty little cruelties in prison wards. . . . Remember that world you planned beyond the southern mountains? It's still a possible world."

"This disease of mine is merely agoraphobia, of course. It'll pass."

"Then—?"

"Of course." He caught her hand and stood up with her. He winced at his straining clothes, as she did. Clair's laughter had survived Atlantis. He shook her, very gently. "We could never do anything else, I suppose— even though we bring a flint spear against a sixteen-inch gun."

THEY stood together in the sunset. The sea rumbled again at their feet in the beat of the incoming tide. And out for miles, hasting into the west, the fading light leaped from roller to roller of the Atlantic. Remote above them the culvert belched out another train to sweep the mountain track down to San Miguel.

Sinclair's hand fell on Clair's.

THE END

GALAXY MAGAZINE
and
SIMON and SCHUSTER
announce
The Richest Science Fiction
Novel Contest in History

$6500
minimum
Guaranteed to the author of the best
ORIGINAL Science Fiction Novel Submitted

... To raise the literary level of the field still higher ...

... To augment the already high standards with new writing talent ...

... To focus more attention on this increasingly important form of literature.

Galaxy Science Fiction Magazine and one of the leading book publishers, Simon and Schuster, Inc. have joined to offer by far the LARGEST CASH PRIZE ever awarded a science fiction novel.

The author of the prize-winning novel will receive AT LEAST $6500 in outright cash gifts, payments and guaranteed advance royalties.

... The award novel will appear as a serial in Galaxy Science Fiction Magazine ...

... It will be published in book form by Simon and Schuster ...

... It will be republished in pocket size by Dell Publishing Co.

The prize-winning author will thus receive a GUARANTEED MINIMUM of $5500 for the purchase of First World serial and T.V. rights by Galaxy Science Fiction Magazine and guaranteed advance royalties for book and reprint publication ... plus AN OUTRIGHT GIFT of $1000.

The entire $6500 award will be paid to the winner at the time his (or her) name is announced—certainly the largest single payment to any author in the history of science fiction.

Here are the details and rules of the $6500 Galaxy Magazine and Simon and Schuster Science Fiction contest

1. The closing date is October 15, 1953. Manuscripts may be submitted at any time prior to that date and sent to NOVEL CONTEST, Galaxy Science Fiction, 421 Hudson Street, New York 14, N. Y.

2. Manuscripts must be ORIGINAL (never before published in any form) and not committed to any other magazine or book publisher.

3. Novels submitted must be between 60,000 and 75,000 words in length, typed in black ink on one side of white bond paper, double-spaced, with at least an inch margin on all sides and each page numbered.

4. Manuscripts must be accompanied by sufficient postage for return.

5. There will be only ONE winner, but all other submissions of merit will be given full consideration for possible serialization in Galaxy Science Fiction Magazine, book publication by Simon and Schuster, or both, at standard rates.

6. There are no requirements, stipulations or taboos regarding themes. Fresh ideas and convincing characterization, conflict and plot development are the important criteria. Writers who enter the contest can best familiarize themselves with the standards of the judges through study of the science fiction published by Galaxy Science Fiction Magazine and Simon and Schuster.

7. Sole judges will be the editorial staffs of Galaxy Science Fiction Magazine and Simon and Schuster. The decisions of the judges will be final.

8. Contestants agree, in submitting their manuscripts, to accept standard publishing agreements with the sponsors of the contest in the event that their novel is the winning entry.

9. Anyone may enter this contest except employees of the Galaxy Publishing Corp. and of Simon and Schuster, Inc., and their families; AND authors who are ineligible because of contractual obligations to their present publishers . . . which means, in effect, that contestants will NOT be competing with most of the established "big names" of science fiction.

www.ingramcontent.com/pod-product-compliance
Lightning Source LLC
Chambersburg PA
CBHW020146180626
46810CB00004B/1758